FOREWARD

This book is the first of a two-part adventure that was inspired by several of my work slaves. While I had coffee on the left coast at the San Francisco Bay, one suggested I set this story in a remote location a few hundred miles from the Bay and pointed "thataway" toward an island reachable only by boat. Another boy encouraged me to relate the details about the way I train my work slaves – both male and female – into proper workers. A third suggested I specify the training rules for my new slaves and let you, the reader, know that once you are hired by Mistress Amity, she will own you – body, soul and fears – for the rest of your life. Some of their suggestions were useful and make up some of the background of the story you are about to read. There is no reason for me to make up fiction if my reality suffices. I train my work slaves to perform the way I demand, and it is indeed for the rest of their lives.

Welcome to my Company and meet some of the slaves who work for me. And be sure to keep your eye on interesting want ads.

CONTENTS

INTRODUCTION

Owning a large business with multiple divisions and locations has challenges and the one constant of those trials is finding exceptional staff and training them to work for me within my rules and processes. Once trained and performing to my expectations, I keep the boy workers forever. It did not take long for me to see that males – when properly trained – make decent workers. Women, who likewise require proper training that rises to my expectations, make more effective supervisors and managers.

This story, the first of two parts, includes actual training techniques used at my Company, processes that make sure work they perform is done exceptionally well, on time and at or under budget. That is what makes my Company such a success. My experience shows that careful hiring, excellent training, and unrelenting demands that my goals are met is how I achieve that success.

I place an occasional want ad to find the male slaves whose skills are what I need. Boys that I accept to interview must survive our processes and adhere to Company procedures. It is not surprising that none of them ever leave. I allow a few to retire, but I still own them: body, soul, and fears. My few females are managers who excel at keeping the boys' work product perfect. You will learn what I look for in new hires throughout this story. You will feel the unyielding hand I keep clenched around every facet of my Company and the boys who produce for me.

Take a deep breath and join my train on its trek to the Company HQ. Join in the severe training and see if you could endure it and eventually submit to my authority absolutely. And most of all, read the online want ads from time to time to try to find my special want ad. You never know where it will take you. But you can find out in Part 2, coming soon.

i

The CEO

Bent over with their asses spread wide, their voices shrieking insanely through gagged mouths and their bodies spasming in delightful synchronicity, the new boys' antics were ignored by Company Medical staff, who pierced the five new hires between their cock and balls and assholes. They attached electronic rings and locked them permanently in place. They swiftly initialized the microchips. From her vantage point, the CEO nodded.

She kept a keen eye on her staff at all times through her multi-monitor setup and she particularly enjoyed mass piercing and subsequent branding of new hires. It showed that Intake was about to begin in earnest. The train trek was over and the boys – and a few new females – were ready to join her Company's ranks.

The CEO's iron fist of ownership gripped the entire staff. During the Company's 20-year history, no boy had ever escaped.

The Want Ad

CREATIVE FIRM HIRING ON-SITE STAFF

Are you willing to give up your old ideas about how a business is run and embrace our new discipline? Are you seeking a real lifestyle change? We are a well-established multi-facility creative company hiring more out-of-the box thinkers for careers at our headquarters. Our currently available positions include: Corporate Executive, HR Professional, IT Security Engineer, Web Developer, and a Trained Plumber. Work and live on-site. Generous personal and professional benefits for those who make the cut. Five-year commitment required. Are you ready to give up your old ideas about how a successful business is run and to submit to a different kind of Company discipline? If that's you and what you want and need, click here to upload your resume.

Growing her company was the CEO's favorite sport, and she enjoyed hiring and especially training new staff. When business grew, she needed new hires and the ones she chose were screened in excruciating detail before they were trained how to work painfully and efficiently. She always placed an attractive Want Ad when it was time to bring in new workers.

Chapter 1

The Want Ad ran only one week.

IN SILICON VALLEY

Ever since Evan got into highly successful venture capital forays, he scoured the weekend specialty employment ads to see which new firms were growing and hiring. The number and type of ads he read provided him fascinating information for his "maybe" list of investments that led ultimately to his takeovers. This Sunday morning, he was at his desk sipping a just-delivered latte and glancing at ads that caught his eye. One ad jumped out at him.

Lifestyle change? That was certainly different from the usual ads, he mused. Ideas flashed in and out of his thoughts while he considered just what kind of business this company might be engaged in. He clicked to view the online application and the black/white/grey color scheme he saw seemed too conservative for a company promising a *real* lifestyle change. But one question grabbed his attention.

Maybe it was the bold font in this sentence:

> *Are you ready to give up your old ideas about how a successful business is run and to submit to a different kind of Company discipline?*

His cock reacted first and he knew at that moment that he had to find out more. If this ad was a recruiting tool for the kind of lifestyle he occasionally paid for and if that meant this company was unafraid to advertise for a business dealing with domination and sex somehow might succeed, then he was definitely interested. One of the luxuries of buying, breaking up and selling off companies was that Evan could investigate off-beat possibilities and decide when he wanted to destroy them for a profit. Added to that was Evan's proclivities. He had paid for many first-rate Domme/sub sex play sessions and he craved more first-rate experiences. Besides, he could afford to indulge his pleasures.

What the heck, he thought and filled out the online application. His answers to each question made his cock bulge bigger. When he was done, Evan staggered into the bathroom and jerked himself off. The explosion was amazing. He was having a great Sunday morning.

He never expected to hear from the company – if that was what it really was – again.

IN BROOKLYN

Across the country on the east coast, James huddled in a cold studio apartment in an area of not-yet-gentrified Brooklyn and cupped his hands around the only unchipped coffee cup he owned. It steamed with the boring scent of instant coffee. He was online extra early this morning because sleep was hard to come by since his release. Trying to find a job with a felony conviction and prison time for rape and sexual assault on his record consumed James's waking hours. He read every want ad, no matter in what skill section they were published.

Then he saw the CEO's want ad.

Discipline jumped out at him. After a ten-year incarceration, James wanted a new lifestyle and prison therapy taught him that his crimes – rape and assault – gave him a professional life-ending conviction unless he found a new way of controlling his anger toward the woman who had told him to get fucked and get out of her life. The therapist told him over and over that the only way he would stay out of prison was to submit his anger toward women to the control of a strong, positive boss at work and only then would he be able to establish a meaningful personal or professional relationship.

He thought she was full of shit. But the conditions of his parole were clear: he could work anywhere, but he had to work and present a monthly paycheck stub to the parole officer who was another pain-in-his-ass controlling woman. James was pretty sure they assigned him to her on purpose, just to make him angry. But he was a certified plumber with the help of work-study in prison and if anyone could use a lifestyle change, then it was him.

His court-ordered therapist had verbally smacked him around routinely, James remembered, and she forced him to agree with her about that strong women thing. He hated her but with every verbal slap she planted on his face, his penis pounded and helped him forget her controlling personality. James knew that he just needed a woman to fuck, and that would fix his penis problem. He was tired of using his own hands.

James began filling out the application and for the first time he could remember after those ten awful years, he did not care at all in what city he would wind up. There was nothing for him in Brooklyn anymore. When he finished the application, he hobbled toward the toilet and jerked off with an intensity that made him grin. But he still wanted a woman. Any woman.

IN AUSTIN TEXAS

In a three-bedroom, two-bath rental house in Texas, Henry clicked next, next, next in the browser and glanced at each job before he would dutifully return to his own personal website and update the photos and post a few prurient new articles. His only source of income was that darned website and unless he kept his mostly male membership sexually aroused with prick teasing pornography, he would not be able to pay this month's rent. The porn website seemed like an easy idea at the time for fast money, so Henry used his web development skills that he learned at the last job he was fired from to build a site for men who, like himself, longed for good-looking women to pay attention to them.

Women, especially pretty ones, were all over his landscape, but Henry had no luck getting one for himself. Just like his online incel subscribers, women were brutal to him and looked past him at every bar or club he went to trying to find a woman for sex. He began hating them – mostly the nicer-looking ones – but he hated the men they attached themselves to even more. Men just like him were pretty much the personality of his membership, which is why Henry's site was chock full of new members every month and his rent got paid.

But the lifestyle change and especially the discipline offered in the want ad made him look twice. Moving somewhere for five years rent-free and finally having good medical insurance seemed almost too good to be true. It could not hurt, he figured, to apply online. He had nothing of value to lose. He did not even own the furniture in his rental house and moving would be easy.

He began filling out the form.

After the first page of pretty general contact information, Henry found himself struggling to choose between yes and no on the longer question list. Each question made him want the advertised web job even more, so he wanted his answers to line up with the likely expectations of the hiring firm. He desperately wanted a callback at least.

> When your boss tells you to get this done today, would you stay late a work to finish even if she were leaving early for a dinner date?

Henry sucked up his real feelings and checked "yes."

> If your boss told you she thought you should dress and groom better, would you take her advice?

Henry sputtered into his coffee at the audacity of the question, but his rent was due next week and he clicked the "yes" button again.

> The woman who has the private office in your
> section and approves your raises and promotions
> is criticizing your work. Would you report her to
> her boss?

Henry gritted his teeth and checked "no."

And so, his morning slipped by as he checked what he thought were the preferred answers to make sure he got contacted about this job. After the final annoying question, he clicked "Submit" and sneered at the woman behind the job in the want ad that he wanted so desperately, who was forcing him to say the opposite of what he felt. He hated her, too.

IN PARIS

The sun was setting across the winding Seine that Cory saw every morning when he drank café au lait in his left-bank corporate apartment. He was in the third year and nearly at the end of the final phase of his assignment in France and knew that he needed to start boxing up his personal belongings to return to the US and see what this project's success would mean for his career back home. He supposed his accomplishments would be rewarded by the C-suite actors at the national office, but he also realized that nothing in Cleveland could ever compare to the joie de vivre he enjoyed in Paris.

The women in Paris were *easy*, he found out, and he knew how to work them. All he had to do was stand up to his full six-foot four-inch height, flash his championship ring and let them wonder exactly how toned his abs were under his custom-made dress shirts. Cory never lacked for a woman on any weekend and within two months of arriving, he could count on finding one for any weeknight he chose. French women loved tall, athletic African American men.

The prospect of leaving Paris and returning to Cleveland filled Cory with emptiness. You can never go home again, he sighed, as he checked out the want ads that might lead him in another direction.

Lifestyle caught his eye. So did the *five-year commitment*. To an HR professional like himself, full benefits were very attractive. His eyes wandered to the link and on a whim, he clicked it. Cory read the form's overview page and to his surprise, he started filling it out. The second page's questions jumped out at him and his trained eye did not miss the gender references. This was a woman-owned company, he surmised, and seeing how easily he conquered the women of Paris, he figured he would be on a fast track in a firm like this. Besides, he thought, I would have to go in with a big title.

Cory clicked to page three and saw the rating matrix. What he did not realize was that the questions changed dynamically based his answers on the previous page.

On a scale of 1-10, with 1 being the least likely and 10 being the most likely, respond to each:

> Your boss put you in charge of a long-term project. It is nearly done but the text needs some massaging. How likely is it that you will do those edits, or you will leave them for her?

His first inclination was to give it a "1" because the bitch could do it herself, but he gave in and entered an "8" because he wanted to know more about the job. The next question caught his eye.

> A male co-worker invites you to dinner and you think he is attracted to you. Your female boss has encouraged you to interact more with your co-workers. She offers her private club membership for dinner. How likely is it that you will accept the invitation?

That was a thought that Cory always pressed to the back of this mind, but it jumped into front-and-center space right now. A guy?

Doing it with a guy? Cory thought he had suppressed those feelings, but his twitching penis and hot balls brought them all rushing back.

Each of the ensuing questions rang a bell with Cory's take on the what the implications of his answers would be to the company's HR department. Even though he was experienced in HR applications, this set of questions made him think twice about his replies. With each new question, he tried to outsmart the not-so-subtle implications and balance his replies. But each time he clicked "next" on the screen, he could not go back to change or review what he had said, and he worried that he wouldn't be open enough for the firm's apparently very special culture. As the questions appeared on his screen, he felt rising urgency to get them right and tried to ignore the telltale drip of excitement he knew was glistening on the tip of his penis.

Damn, he thought, he was getting hot from an online form.

> Your superior sprained her ankle playing tennis and you are working late. You are the only two people in the office. How likely is it that you will offer to massage her injured ankle?

He took a deep breath and clicked the "10."

IN SAN FRANCISCO

Every Sunday morning, Oliver straightened up his desk that spanned most of the long wall in his home office. He was a neat freak and he rarely let it get out of hand with paper or files, but he liked seeing the shiny desktop with each monitor unencumbered by coffee cups or staplers. The idea of a stapler always made him smile. With so much cloud storage, Oliver had not kept much paper in the past five years but always kept a stapler handy on his otherwise bare workspace.

He enjoyed working at home. With no commute, he did not put miles on his car or have to buy a work wardrobe. Most of all, he did not have to contend with co-workers. Ever since he was written up for making an unprofessional comment to a subordinate, a gal he was convinced had been hired because she was female and not mostly because she came from a first-rate school, Oliver preferred the telecommute option he was offered. He could manage servers and routers from just about anywhere and did not have to talk to people except through Slack where he could block video and not have to endure their faces.

But the one thing that bothered him every day of his telecommuting life was the lower pay. He knew that other guys he graduated with were making more – especially after thumbing through the alumni directory and seeing their beach and mountain houses – and Oliver believed he was being victimized for that one episode at work with that damned woman and the write-up that followed. After that, on the weekends he usually went through the higher-level want ads for experienced network and security administrators using a laptop that was air gapped and formatted regularly. One thing that Oliver was always careful about was who could track his online history, like the occasional story he read about female dominants or the male slave and bondage pictures he visited on sites he would have blocked for other users at work.

He happened onto the CEO's want ad in the "career and lifestyle positions" section and paused for a deeper look. His fingers tapped keys almost on their own accord and once he finished entering his contact information, the proficiency matrix caught his attention.

> Rate yourself on a scale of 1-10 for each type of hardware and/or software.

Oliver read through the list and began salivating. This firm had state-of-the-industry that Oliver wished he could start playing with and tweak.

He finished all the questions and clicked submit. His mouse moved to his hidden bookmarks and he clicked one that made his cock drip. Oliver was silent except for an occasional grunt when the hand he was using to jerk off touched one of his favorite spots. He knew it was not "that" small, as the last girl he fucked had said those long two years ago.

Chapter 2

The applicants were warned during the oral and video interviews that getting to their new home at the Company for their five year commitment was a long journey and started with a two-day train trek to its remote location. Evan thought it was odd that they did not just hire a private jet to transport the new hires and was not looking forward to spending two days in his own compartment aboard a noisy, rattling and technologically unsophisticated conveyance. But he salivated at the idea that within a few weeks he would figure out whether this intriguing business model was worth buying out from under this upstart woman who probably had barely a tenth of the business skills that he amassed in his years of buying, breaking up and selling businesses.

James was looking forward to having his own tiny compartment on the overnight train to wherever the destination was. Having spent too many years behind bars in the tight company of whomever the warden assigned as his cellmate, James was elated at having hot food delivered to him and his own recliner chair that he saw during the interview video. It was far better and more comfortable than where he was living now.

If the train had decent WiFi, then Henry was in favor of having a couple of days to catch up on whatever Google suggested and was already working on searches that would provide interesting reading, especially about new trends in UX layouts and a couple of APIs he wanted to check out. And maybe a kinky website or two.

Oliver did not care one whit about the train ride; instead, he could not wait to get his hands on the bleeding-edge tools and servers that were displayed in the video interview. He saw a few women IT engineers working on them, but he was sure they were probably misconfiguring them. After all, they were highly complex machines.

For his part, Cory rescheduled his flight to Cleveland and set up a second flight that let him have three days for the in-person interview that home office would never know about until he got the job. He had seen other companies fill their websites with female gender pronouns but this one was unusual in that even the test questions referred only to women. They could certainly use his skills to upgrade the questions and be more neutral in how they presented themselves. They obviously needed him to manage Human Resources.

The five of them – each with his own personal plan for the two-day train trek – arrived as directed exactly at 6am on a Wednesday morning at the designated downtown building. As instructed, each used a ride-share service, paid for it with the preconfigured app they were instructed to download and emerged suitcase-less outside the front door.

They checked each other out.

It was surprising to Evan that they arrived almost simultaneously, and he noted that whoever the CEO was – she was alluded to by all his interviewers, but interestingly never by name – managed to get their arrivals scheduled correctly. He eyeballed the other four men and noticed that they were eyeballing him back. Except for one black guy who seem uninterested in anyone else in the group.

No one wanted to be the first to speak so Evan nodded at the first guy who looked like his income could compare to his own. Cory tilted his head once in Evan's direction. *A potential cognac-drinking buddy*, Evan thought when a blaring speaker interrupted his plan.

"Inside," a woman's voice said curtly. "One at a time through the revolving door."

James wasted no time in entering the building first and the other four were stunned as the door spun a partial rotation and suddenly stopped. That's when they noticed that the glass panes had turned opaque.

"Next!" the voice commanded as the door began to spin again.

Henry's legs carried him into the dark door's available opening and the three remaining men watched as the scene repeated. The door stopped for a few moments and the voice ordered the next to step in.

Next to dare to enter was Oliver, followed by Cory. Finally, Evan stood by himself on the sidewalk and waited for the unmoving door to start to spin again so he could enter. The women inside observed him as he took an impatient few steps this way and that, always returning to the exact sidewalk square on which he started. He looked up at the speaker from which the voice had spoken but with his face saying, "get on with it" and finally morphed into an impatient look of "It's my turn, hurry up."

The women in charge of entry knew there would always be one like this boy in new-hire groups. This time his name was Evan.

As he stared at the silent speaker, he never saw three women move behind him and pin his arms. They swiftly cuffed his wrists behind his back with plastic zip strips. When the black bag was slipped over his head, he felt that much outrage since the woman he fired had secretly bought the majority shares in the company he had just acquired and threw him out as CEO.

Chapter 3

Wherever the five of them landed was warm and dark. The four revolving door entrants stood in a windowless room and waited for instructions. James was the only calm one of the foursome but he was used to waiting for orders. Henry, Cory, and Oliver fidgeted and paced. Behind the cameras, every one of their moves was observed and noted. Bringing new boy hires into the Company followed a tested set of rules and although this quintet included a few new types of boy hirelings, the Intake staff was looking forward to measuring and training them according to their CEO's techniques.

The women knew that all male hires came to the train trek with their own psychological baggage. Boys had bad habits that had to be erased and most new hires acted according to their own false ideas that the Company knew required erasing and replacing with correct ones. Although all the Intake staff would enjoy providing their CEO with the five new skillsets she demanded, the Trainers often joked that breaking them down before official training began and moving them up to Company standards was the most fun they had in their careers at the Company.

Sybil tapped her tablet and the staff moved into action. Each Intake staff member hurried to her dressing area and donned the supplied outfit. Within minutes, the staff was dressed in business suits, stiletto heels and garter-pinned stockings. Their faces were carefully made up especially for their roles. They each wrapped their hair into a tight bun. When Sybil inspected and approved them, the women were set loose onto the new hires.

Four women strode into the dark room and walked around the men like predators circling their prey. Cory cleared his throat to speak and

Chloe put her fingers to her lips to tell him wordlessly, "Quiet." Cory stared at her in disbelief.

"You shushed me?" he asked, his voice rising in anger.

Chloe stared back at him, her eyes rising slightly above her glasses, as the women wondered just how long it would take her to train this one into silence. It usually took her three or four times before a new boy understood to keep his mouth shut. They were rooting for her to break that record.

Cory would have none of it. His recent stint in Paris had taught him that demanding what he wanted from women got him exactly that. He took a step toward Chloe to let his requirements be known.

"I want to know exactly what's going on here," he started. "And I want to know now!"

Some will start with a demand. At the Company, boys are not allowed to have demands. Train them to have no expectations.

Chloe attributed her success in her job to two things: recognizing the problem and fixing it swiftly. In what looked like a single motion, she pulled a taser from her belt and pressed it to the back of Cory's knee. Within seconds, he was writhing on the floor while the three other new hires watched in horror.

Henry gasped aloud and Cassandra approached him, her finger to her lips. Without speaking a word, she dominated him into silence. He took one step backwards and she knew from that physical retreat that he would be one of the easier ones to break in training. She pushed him into the wall and pressed his shoulders against it. His quadriceps ached as his feet were still several inches away from it. He struggled to remain upright.

But Oliver did not learn from either lesson and began ranting.

"Wait just a minute!" he yelled as Sybil noted this outspokenness on her tablet. "That's not right – how DARE you tase him? I do not think…"

Before he finished that sentence, Casey jammed her hand between his legs, pulled and squeezed in a well-practiced motion and watched him tumble to the floor. Still holding his cock and balls like a prize bull about to be castrated, she lifted his backside at least three inches off the tile floor. As was usual with this type of nerdy IT-security-complex hire, Oliver kept on screaming.

She lifted his ass higher off the floor.

After a few minutes of his pointless and noisy protest, Oliver fell silent in a mix of outrage and pain. That was when Sybil noted that Casey's achievement set a new record for this Intake group and entered the new time on her tablet. The CEO would be pleased.

It is not just getting to the goal I demand. It must be done quickly and decisively. Lessons must be learned in seconds, not days.

That left James standing silently as Claudia approached him. What a nice piece of ass, he mused for a moment. With one leg, she cut his knees out from under him and he flopped to the tile floor. At the Company, boys were not allowed to even think such thoughts.

Chapter 4

On her monitor, Cara saw Sybil nod and she grabbed Evan's zip cuffs. Pulling him by his locked wrists, she marched him into the Intake collection room. The four new hires were quite a sight – two on the floor moaning and writhing, one backed up against a wall with a woman pressing his shoulders into the wallboard and the last one flopping noiselessly in the middle of the room. Evan did not see any of it through the black bag that covered his head.

Sybil was ready for the new hires to be boarded on the train and ran her checklist so the five boys and their Intake trainers could ready them for transport. This was one of her favorite rapid-fire training scenarios. She spoke into her headset's microphone as her staff listened on their ear comms.

"Bag the rest. Put the transport cuffs on," she barked.

The Intake trainers were happy to hand off the group to the Transport Team that would move them from the building to the train depot. They slid black bags over the heads of their charges and laced the drawstrings. With an expert flourish, they slipped wrist restraints on the foursome and locked them in place. The zip cuffs were proven effective in preventing falls or an occasional failed escape attempt. Sybil activated the cuffs, including Evan's, and the boys were secured. Each Trainer was electronically locked to her trainee and any untoward moves by the new hires would result in a quick and effective full-body jolt.

The new hires would be implanted as soon as they got to HQ in a procedure that the HR trainers enjoyed. Until they were implanted, they women were completely in charge of their males and could use any means they chose to transport them to the train. Their CEO was clear: *by any means.*

Get them on the train with single-word commands. That is your goal. And that's what you are trained to accomplish.

The five men had no idea what the metal zip cuffs on their wrists did beyond restraining them, but four had experienced exactly what these women were capable of doing to them so they did not dare test them. The march from Intake to the transport bus that would take them to the train usually played out without incident but some trips were memorable both for what some of these new hires attempted to do as well as for what the Intake staff was capable of doing to them to make sure they achieved the training goal.

Sybil readied herself for the trek and all its possibilities. The Intake trainers grasped their male's cuffs and waited for her to order them to begin. The trainers could feel their boys' tension through the cuffs and each steadied herself to expect – and react – to almost anything.

Claudia recalled a trek to the train a few years ago when a straggling new hire tried to lag behind the group and then try to trip her during his transport trek. Her lips curled when she ran the scenario through her mind and remembered how she used her gloved hand to grab the male's cock and pierce the skin with its claws that bulged from two of the glove's fingertips. His surprised shriek entertained her for the duration of that transport trek.

Chloe and Cassandra shared a team memory when it took two of them to corral a big bull – a new hire who, it turned out, was later trained into a decent male exercise assistant. His trek included an insulting *"Suck my cock!"* remark to Chloe who immediately checked with Cassandra. The last thing that male saw before the black bag covered his head was Cassandra reaching for his ass and piercing it with a thin metal rod. He felt it crush between his cheeks and up his anus before his rectum flared as if on fire as a highly effective chemical was discharged inside him. He screamed throughout the entire transport trek to the bus and whimpered during the flight to the train. The other new hires had no idea what had been done to him – but they knew whatever that was should be avoided at all cost. He managed to crawl to the transport bus and that was Chloe's goal all along. The goal was all that mattered.

Ever since that experience, all males were now marched naked on their trek to bus that took them to the train. It was easier that way.

Intake training was one important phase of the new hire program that the CEO was particularly partial to growing. She was unrelenting in training her trainers and improving their techniques to develop the staff she required. Before every new hire season, they were trained again and provided new tools for the transport trek. After each season, Trainers met with the Company's design team and all the engineers to discuss the effectiveness of each tool and share their suggestions for new ones.

Casey was the Intake Trainer that Sybil, who ran the HR Intake unit, counted on most for fresh ideas. The mini-taser was one of Casey's suggestions as was the idea to taper the wrist restraints so that even if a new hire were willing to break his thumbs, he could not slip it off. It was also one of her better esthetic choices to replace the red, orange, and green buttons they used with blue ones of different hues. The CEO believed that color both increased function and had more attractive eye-appeal. She appreciated ideas that improved Intake but she kept a few of the old colors that she preferred.

The newest addition to the Trainers' bags of training tools was the re-engineered implant that would be inserted into the new hires' cocks when they reached the train. Although they always used cock control tools, the CEO constantly improved them. They ranged from external lock-on cages to electronic inventions that were activated by buttons on the trainers' bodices and tablets to the newest iteration: permanent cock titanium rods that were to be threaded into this quintet for the first time in the Company's history. It was one surprise they would get when they reached HQ.

Casey could not wait for watch – and listen – to that.

Chapter 5

With the five new hires' wrists secured in metal cuffs and their clothing unceremoniously removed, the Intake staff herded them into the freight elevator and rode 12 floors down to the lowest level of the parking garage. The CEO leased all the spaces on that level so there were no inquisitive outsiders watching how the staff performed this step in the trek to the transport bus. The bus, its engine expectantly idling, would haul them in silence to the train depot for their two-day trip to HQ. In prior years, they had issues with some of the new hires whose reading comprehension of the want ad's specifications left a lot for them to learn.

The CEO knew that many new hires were reluctant to step into open air when their clothes were confiscated black bags were tied over their heads. This group proved to be no different. Cory's handler snapped the lock on the steel belt she had wrapped around his middle on the elevator ride and because she was in the front, she knew she would have to move him quickly through the parking garage to the bus so the rest could follow in a timely manner. It was always more challenging to be the first Trainer during the first single-word command lesson.

The elevator doors wooshed open. Cory stood motionless when he felt the cool air. Even though he could not see through the black bag, he knew he had arrived in a place that was outside. And he was not taking a willing step into it.

Chloe was masterful at making reluctant new hires move how and when she wanted. Cory would be easy, she guessed. She had been taught that the fewer words used, the better the training experience.

She needed to achieve "single-word" obedience and she relished making Cory follow her orders.

Slipping her fingers between the steel belt and his dark brown skin, Chloe tugged once to spur him to take a first step. He refused to obey her physical command. She tugged again. When he still did not move at all, she chose a tried-and-true technique she perfected during past new hire sessions.

"Walk!" she said and made a single syllable her only command. She simultaneously jerked Cory's cock in the direction she wanted him to move.

The rest of the new hires saw none of Chloe's talent with transport trek techniques. Instead they only heard Cory yelp in pain. Hidden from their bag-covered eyes, Cory stepped onto the parking garage's concrete floor, almost falling over his own feet in his eagerness to comply and remove the painful grip she had on his cock.

Chloe's lips never smiled. She knew this would be the last time she would repeat a command to this new boy. As she cock-tugged him toward the bus, she glanced behind her to see if the others were following. Her eyebrows rose when she saw Cassandra raise her foot and aim it at Henry's cock and balls.

Apparently, Henry had not listened well.

He was a particularly hairy one, Chloe noticed. Throughout her years of experience in Intake, she came to see the link between hairy men and reluctance to comply with training orders. One day, she would think about writing an article about it for the Company newsletter. But today, she watched Cassandra closely so she could provide complete answers to the questions she was going to be asked during the debrief that always followed Intake.

Henry's background check revealed his overt dislike of women in authority. He had a couple of run-ins with senior graphics staff at two companies when his web designs were criticized, and one was rejected outright. One interviewee they talked to during background checks conveyed to the staff that not only did Henry call his female supervisor rude names but also made disrespectful gestures behind her back. Even worse, he once dared to add hidden code into a website that disparaged her hairstyle.

Henry was going to learn his place before he would fit into his role in the Company. That was what the Intake staff's single-word command training process was designed to accomplish.

For Henry, this transport trek was not going to be a simple cock-grab-and-pull, Cassandra knew. Her new hire was going to require more effective and long-lasting instruction.

Once. Give your Single-Word Command only once. Make them obey it immediately. It shall become the boy's eternal command.

With a quick snap she grabbed a long tool on her bodice and pulled it off its Velcro attachment. Cassandra chose a rectal lube injector for this trek and inserted it straight into Henry's unsuspecting ass. When it was in place, she released the fluid. Before he could scream wildly from his outrage at having his ass invaded, she removed it but not before depositing a polished chrome capsule deep inside his anal cavity. The demonic device had several tail feathers that hung out and fluttered behind his scrawny legs.

When she pressed the light blue button on her training vest, Henry screamed and lurched forward. The bag covering his head muted the agonized sound a little but the new hire behind him heard it clearly. His little dangling penis quivered in fear as Henry repeatedly shrieked and lurched toward the bus as Cassandra's finger tapped the light blue button whenever she felt like he needed more encouragement.

One of their most effective inventions, the long-tailed ass capsule, was harmless looking until the light blue button was pressed. Then the capsule radiated a stinging pain that made the wearer feel like his ass was going to explode. When the Trainer stopped it, most new hires obeyed whatever they had been instructed to do. Perhaps out of fear. But it did not matter. It was all about the obedience.

Focused pain replaces a thousand words. If a single word does not bring out the proper behavior, use pain. Be fast. Make it effective.

That was why the Intake team always required the Trainers to do the transport trek to the waiting bus one-by-one. Each Trainer wanted to be sure her new hire followed her single word command the first time and made certain that her voice was clear. Cara glanced at Claudia and motioned to her to move her boy to the transport bus.

Claudia thought about using her rattan cane on James's short thick cock as a backup to a single word command but knew that he was used to obeying orders from his prison experience. That posed a training quandary because she expected immediate obedience, of course, but she demanded that James perform her instructions not just from a routine he learned in jail. Her goal for this new hire was an authentic experience and total submission to *her* and not just a habit of submitting to authority.

James remained unfazed through the others' screams, shrieks and audible sobs. It was as if the new hires' pain and suffering did not touch him at all. Claudia knew that to be trained for the Company, she would have to make James feel deep inside that he was an equal member of the new class – no better and no worse. The group would succeed or fail together. It was the Company way.

She decided to make her first command intensely personal. He had to *feel* her unique authority deep inside his gut.

Claudia chose a training tool that had not been used in the past two or three seasons of incoming classes – a basic hog tie. Designed by the CEO for group control, it was used from time to time when a big bull or an especially hardened new hire needed fast and effective discipline. Besides, the CEO enjoyed watching the biggest boys flop around on their bellies when she had them hog tied for a few minutes' amusement.

She snapped two of the hog tie's rings around James's ankles, threw him to the parking garage floor and pulled his manacled hands behind him. Then she secured each through the two remaining loops. With a tap of the medium blue button on her bodice, the rings tightened, and James looked like a fat farm hog being prepped for slaughter. Claudia placed her black boot squarely on his ass and pushed.

James' chunky frame rolled over and she pressed her foot into his ass again.

He rolled grotesquely toward the bus each time her boot laid into him. With each rotation, the clank of metal rings against the concrete parking garage floor filled the quiet air. Claudia moved her foot to his cock, stepped hard and pushed again. James screamed as he was forced to roll again.

James' jerking rolling across the concrete was not enough for Claudia – she needed him to understand that he was not just rolling on the parking garage floor. He had to comprehend that he rolled only because she told him to roll. She gave him a single word command.

"Roll."

And he did. Like a hooked fish flopping on the wet boat deck, James forced his body to swivel and contract and extend so it would force his considerable size to roll. He rolled once and stopped in exhaustion.

She repeated the single word. "Roll." And he made it happen again.

Claudia was confident that the big ex-con whose background check revealed the times he fixed pipes and leaks in exchange for having his ass beaten with a whip by a woman who the CEO had hired to take explicit video, was now responding directly to her. The Intake staff entered a mental check next to this new boy's single word command training achievement.

It was Casey's turn on the transport trek.

Although he had seen none of it, Oliver heard every scream and shriek as Cory, Henry and James were forced to the bus. His stomach churned as he listened to the clank of metal on concrete as James rolled like a pig on command. Oliver was sure he did not want whatever had happened to the others to happen to him and decided to comply with whatever he was told to do. He was relieved to feel the outside air on his naked skin and get out of the confines of the elevator. Small places were not his favorite place to be sequestered.

The Intake staff learned from his background check that Oliver was claustrophobic, and they knew that fear could be used to train him more efficiently for the Company. Casey gave the single word command, but Oliver remained immobile. She decided against an anal lesson on his transport trek and mentally ran through the options she had at the ready to achieve the only acceptable response he could make. Oliver had to get out of the elevator and begin his trek to the bus. Right now.

She chose a two-stage isolater.

The isolater had overcome two of Cassandra's earlier and stubborn new hires. Afterwards, Cassandra showed the Trainers how to use it during a debrief session. This was the first time she would use the device on a boy by herself.

Her co-workers immediately noticed that Casey was about to try something new. They all paused to watch and held their boys still as the women moved around the parking lot to get the best angle to see.

The isolater was a cock control unit made of three plastic boxes in which a cock and two balls were each encased. When pulled backward and locked up tightly inside their cheeks, the wearers sported only a crease that looked exactly like a pussy. Trainers could yank the device backward between a boy's legs and lock it to his steel belt. When a locked boy tried to walk, everyone saw a small crease where his cock used to be and it reminded him – and everyone who saw it – of a vaginal slit. They never said, "like a girl." Rather, it was "how boys

25

should be castrated." They rigged it to crush its contents on command. It was a very effective device.

Casey pulled the cylinder out of its shrink wrap and yanked his cock through it while she pulled his balls hard and stretched them through the lower opening into their new plastic home.

The penis and balls that dangled from his body were no longer part of Oliver's body and were in the process of becoming just a memory. The isolater did its job and became the new cover for the boy's unattractive penis and the two smallish testicles. The isolater made all make hires feel that their pesky genitals were no longer attached to their bodies. Oliver's first reaction may have been to cry but no one could see tears through the hood and none of trainers cared if he were sobbing behind the black hood. All he knew was that his cock and balls could have been cut off right then and there and they could not do anything about it. All he could feel was that they felt "gone."

But the HR Intake staff noted that his thighs shivered in fear. They knew right then that was his tell; shivering thighs became their new assessment for his training regimen, and they would use it mercilessly during the train trek to HQ. Casey grabbed the isolater's handle that protruded from his ass area and dragged Oliver backward toward the bus. It took four hard pulls to spur his shaking thighs to move. But he finally obeyed.

Casey looked at her co-workers and saw that each one had a slight smile. It was only with that approval that she could relax.

The Intake staff loved unearthing quirky male fears and foibles and using them for faster and more efficient training. There was this one male hire two seasons ago who would break down in tears when his feet were bound so they would tie them up from time to time and force him to hop from his chair to his workspace and back. By the time the tone sounded for the workday to begin, he was sobbing like a baby while trying to explain a point for the proposal that his supervisor had forced to him to describe.

Just last year, they brought in an architect who was so petrified of nipple clamps that they clamped him tightly at wakeup time every day and locked the chain to the floor. As they insisted that he "arise," the single word command issued every morning at dawn, the chain pulled the clamps so they bit into his nipples. The boy yelped uncontrollably through every wakeup ritual that all new hires were forced to memorize and repeat immediately upon being ordered out of bed. They eventually learned their mantra of obedience and recited it daily. Even the nipple clamp boy eventually learned that it was not about clamps; rather, it was about his quiet, instantaneous obedience.

But the one that made all the HR Intake staff remember was the six-pack abs personal trainer whose cock was slightly long and thus became very useful for his training. They'd catch him either covering it with both hands or trying to stroke it to calm himself during difficult training sessions when he thought his Trainers could not see. It took that boy longer than most others to realize that they *always* had video of his every movement.

After he stroked it twice and told his sorrowful cock 'not to worry, it would be all right,' Sybil decided to terminate his cock fascination once and for all. She burst into the room with an electric mini whip and had a personal conversation with his quickly-shriveling penis.

"It will *not* be all right," her voice dripped with sarcasm as she whipped his ball sac and tased his cock repeatedly. Grabbing his balls with her spiked glove, Sybil held them tightly and beat his cock from every angle. That boy's eyes were the wildest that most of the staff had ever witnessed and his near-insane screeching about his now-useless cock made them all laugh out loud.

The Intake staff had experienced almost every imaginable means of making the new hires obey the rules. They had no idea they were going to witness a new one today.

In the parking garage, it was Evan's turn to learn how his trek to the transport but would play out.

Chapter 6

The Transport team underwent several training sessions during which they read the boys' background and psych evaluations to find all the weaknesses that they could exploit. They studied areas of stubbornness that they would need to overcome to produce a new class of properly trained male workers for the expanding Company.

Dealing with Evan was a daily focus in their readiness sessions. The CEO knew that he did not apply to the want ad because he aspired to be a low-level male underling to a smart woman supervisor. She knew that he would appear to be cooperative on the outside but had a sinister motive behind his uncharacteristically acquiescent application. Her investigators documented several of his brutal business dealings and how he had driven other companies into the ground and then bought their remnants only to strip out their former success strategies and take their profits. Several of those rebirthed companies were now owned by women who had to scrape the dregs of their former life's work to try to rebuild their former businesses. He even sued most of them for patent infringements on tools and apps they had previously invented.

The CEO would have none of that. Even though Evan had the potential to be her most difficult new hire, she knew she would prevail; the only question was which set of techniques would bring about that success or if she would have to develop new ways to deal with this new hire.

In her planning his Intake, there was no tool or training method she rejected; no punishment she rebuffed, and she practiced all of them with some throw-away staffers. There was no discipline she did not test. Her sessions were ruthless and she always succeeded no matter how long it took.

The CEO's Psych team constantly evaluated the tools that would be used during the Intake team's single-word command training. The results of those exercises were why Evan was the last to be moved from the elevator to the bus. Cara had attended several sessions with the CEO where the Medical and Psychological teams used a few throw-away junior employees who were instructed to pretend that they had Evan-like personalities. They were coached and then they were handed off to Cara to break.

The Psych team's assessment was that Evan needed a novel combination of discipline and training. The CEO decided that she would break him using Cara as her provider of Intake torture.

One practice boy was trained to brush up against Cara with his naked ass; another to dab his cock cage on her leather shorts. Still another tried to appease her with obedience and then tell a higher boy, who, of course, informed his supervisor that she had done something that never happened. The CEO recognized how destructive Evan-like behavior that her teams predicted could be to her Company and how it might disrupt her workers. It deepened her desire to break him even faster. And harder.

Under the CEO's watchful eye along with ideas dictated by the moment, Cara broke each of the practice boys in rapid succession. Both Cara and the CEO knew that breaking each one over too long a time was not the Company's goal. It had to be completed quickly – and it had to happen in front of other new hires and even a few of the throw-aways. That would make a very effective lesson.

The true check of the Psych and Medical teams' planning would happen in the next few minutes. Cara tingled as she looked at her naked new hire and understood that she was being recorded for later evaluation and debrief. Using this new exercise was a test for her almost as much as it was an event designed specially to break Evan.

She opened the package that had been left for her on the elevator floor. Shaking the item out forcefully, she draped the black rubber suit across Evan's shoulders and let it hang toward the ground. As she had practiced on a throw-away boy under the CEO's direction, she pulled the rubber together in the front, zipped it up and locked it shut.

Evan was completely encased in a full rubber body suit from the neck down. His head was invisible under the black bag. He could not move any part of his body, his fingers could touch nothing, and his arms were secured against his sides. The new hire was completely helpless.

She bent him over by grabbing his hair through the bag and pulling straight down. Stepping around him, she unhooked the ass cover and exposed his two hairy cheeks. Using a metal spreader, she opened his asshole and injected a dose of fire lube. His muffled grunt could have been from his surprise, humiliation or even enjoyment; there was no predicting with this particular boy. Cara let him stand there bent over for a minute, his ass spread and exposed, and let the custom lube begin to spread its sting. His groans were mostly muted by outside street sounds as his ass oozed a few drops of lube onto the elevator floor.

Silently, she pushed a metal rod deeper into his anal cavity and snapped it into place. Squeals and squeaks from Evan's throat greeted the end of the metal rod's journey. Again, Cara was not certain if Evan was horrified or if he were simply enjoying the incursion. You never knew with new boys like him.

As she had practiced with several throw-aways, she pulled out the metal rod slightly just to push it in again, in and out, in and out, according to a carefully timed plan so that Evan could not predict when and if his ass would be violated again and more fire would be released. He grunted and moaned but it was not enough for her; the sounds were not quite right enough for Cara or her CEO's instruction that single-word commands were to be achieved.

Break him. Quickly. With a lesson he will never forget. Be certain he learns the first time.

Cara lifted her boot and shoved the rod deeper into Evan's backside until all she could see were the tail feathers hanging limply from his plugged ass. She smiled when he lost his balance and fell to the elevator floor. That was her cue. Using carefully timed kicks, her boot rolled the black rubber bagged boy across the parking garage's concrete floor toward the bus. When his body came to rest at the bus's steps, she hissed a single word in his ear.

"Up," she said without emotion.

The video that was analyzed later in the Intake debriefing showed that Evan somehow managed to lift himself to his knees and flop his torso onto the first step of the bus's entrance before plopping exhausted in the doorway. His black-suited body now blocked everyone else from climbing aboard. To fix that she opened one eye-slit and let him see the Intake staff's mocking smiles as they each grabbed a piece of his rubber body suit and threw him unceremoniously in the bus's luggage compartment for the trip to the train. After all, with a rod shoved up his ass, he could not sit on a seat. They locked the luggage compartment and adjusted the camera so they could keep an eye him during the trek to the train.

The dildo in his ass remained in place for the 45-minute ride as Cara occasionally pressed a button on her bodice to dose him with more fire to remind him that he was always within her reach. She released the button only when she was convinced his screams were authentic.

Later that evening when the video review was over, Cara requested permission to speak and asked, "Do you think he's really broken?"

The CEO replayed a few final seconds and replied, "Not yet."

Chapter 7

Some of the new hires could walk, while others were hauled by maintenance workers and tossed into individual compartments on the Company train for the two-day trek to HQ. After depositing the five new hires, the maintenance boys unzipped and unlocked them while never making eye contact with them. Their duties were specifically to ensure that each new boy lay naked in his compartment and the entire Company staff, from lowly maintenance to their women superiors, performed the exact task they were assigned – no more and they dared not do any less.

Staff boys removed manacles, unlocked belts, stripped off a cock and ball isolater and finally unzipped Evan's rubber suit. He gasped to taste clean air for the first time in hours.

Then he demanded, "Get that thing out of my ass."

The new hires would soon figure out that every moment of their new lives was recorded but for now, the CEO was most interested in evaluating Evan's demeanor. Her speakers relayed this demand and that told her that he believed he had the authority to instruct her staff boy. He was not *pleading*. That would not do. Not at the Company.

She knew that her maintenance boy would not acknowledge Evan's demand and that he certainly would not remove an ass plug simply on a boy's say-so. She focused on Evan's face to see if he appeared either scared or anxious and did not see enough of either to satisfy her. She continued to study his face for several minutes.

It was time to move to the next level of his Intake training.

In the other compartments, the rest of the new hires were taking in their austere environments. With the black bags removed from their heads, they were all blinking in reaction to the bright fluorescent overhead light. Each looked up and down the four walls of his cell and they realized that the walls did not rise all the way to the train car's ceiling. These were obviously not privacy compartments. Each boy gulped air and waited tensely.

James, recalling his days in prison, assumed the small slot in the door was for food delivery.

Oliver was surprised to see high quality video cameras that were apparently sending images from every angle of his cubicle.

Cory sat on the floor, looked up and saw several rings suspended above his head.

Henry looked at the floor and noticed some compressed areas that looked like his feet could fit into them.

The CEO turned her attention to the screen that was focused on the former venture capitalist's cell. She watched Evan press his face, torso and especially his cock into the cold floor as if to relieve his ass's suffering. She nodded to #34, who recorded the behavior into her tablet that synced instantly with the company's digital personnel records.

This round for the Intake team was complete. Five new hires had made the transport trek to the train where, for the next two days of their journey into the rest of their lives, they would be trained in the Company ways. And each boy would be broken or he would be thrown off the train.

Chapter 8

The CEO waited in her private car at the depot for the trainers and new hires to arrive where her private train was idling. She was pleased to see her trainers again after they had invested so many weeks reading applications, recording hidden video and interviewing potential hires and unbeknownst to them, business and family relations. The background checks ordered by the CEO were intensely personal and thorough. Not only did the CEO discover every detail of their professional lives but she also wanted to investigate every nuance and relationship in their private lives as well.

Her IT team edited gigabytes of video to paint a complete portrait of every boy she considered hiring. They produced comprehensive video stories that weighed heavily on the final recommendations from the staff to the CEO for which boys should be brought into the Company.

She invited her two top staffers to watch the videos – Sybil, her #34, and Cara, her #43, the Trainer who supervised the background checks. After discussing each new hire nominee, #43 narrated the video to make specific points about their investigations. The CEO was interested in several episodes in the video and she asked pointed questions about almost every scene.

"Look at his face," she said as #43 paused the video so that she could listen carefully to her. "He's obviously enjoying what he's doing and it doesn't illustrate his reactions to discipline that he won't enjoy. Explain that to me," the CEO demanded.

#43 expanded on the scene's context.

"He's browbeating that woman, calling her names, his personal assistant, because the gift she sent to his mother that was supposedly from him was not expensive enough. She is explaining how much his mother loved the gift, how she learned about his mother's love of afghan blankets, but he keeps insisting that it should have cost more. Notice that he is smirking. He knows exactly what he is doing, that he is being ridiculous because his mother loved the handmade blanket, but he just will not let go of the cost because his assistant has no defense for that. He enjoys making her feel like crap." #43's information was always succinct and on point.

The CEO frowned. She despised those men who harangued women relentlessly and never saw the larger picture. And worse, most of them did it on purpose.

"We'll let him board," she said. "We will instruct him how to value women."

Weeks later, the CEO observed how #43 put the male's face between an instructor's legs and forced him to inhale her aroma while she tested him on the Company's checklist for new boys in proximity to a Trainer. Each time he gasped for air or answered a detailed question wrong, she re-schooled him on the specifics of the Company rule from the manual and tested him again with his face once more pressed close to the instructor's pussy. Just for extra training, she dragged his head up and down so the instructor's pussy was stimulated and forced him to listen to her *ooh* and *ah* as she became more agitated and knowing his face was merely a replacement for a dildo.

She whipped his stiffening cock and then repeated that he would never experience an erection again. The Company enforced zero tolerance of male erection.

The new boy, a former C-Suite executive in the life he gave up in order to work at the Company, felt his face smash into the pussy as he tried to reply to each question she asked in rapid succession. Cara taught the rule again and demanded that he answer each time. He tried to breathe and speak at the same time, but his nose and lips were filling rapidly. He heard the Trainer moan as his face was used simply to stimulate her clitoris and enhance her excitement. Just as #43 grabbed his head and stared into his eyes that demanded he answer her question about a minor company rule right now, the instructor thrust her pelvis into his face to rub against it and finish her orgasm.

She squirted right into his open mouth.

The CEO smiled at the ingenuity of Cara's training method and had Sybil note it on her tablet. Teaching a boy that he's merely a receptacle was an effective lesson.

The women who worked at the Company as office supervisors, trainers and the CEO's special assistants were carefully selected and even more scrupulously trained. The CEO, busy with overseeing all aspects of the Company's success, rarely had time to learn her women's names, so she had them tagged with how many years they had been with her and a special number that only she knew how to interpret. Numbering them made the CEO's life easier and their brands fit better on their breasts. Sybil, who was recently elevated to #34, made sure each woman at the company was retagged every year on her Company anniversary and the CEO rebranded them annually.

When she demanded one of her trainers or staff to appear, the CEO instructed her assistant to "Get me #75," or "Bring me #62." It was much more efficient that way and no staff ever had a name other than her number at the Company.

The CEO kept a carefully culled lineup of former executives who were reduced to being trainees at the Company to use for her own recreation. Some of them were simply practice objects used in the schooling of new hires. The new boys' tasks were focused completely on learning to work at the Company and were assigned only to benefit the Company. They had no other use.

Chapter 9

The CEO kept a small group of males that were required to supply her personal relaxation. No male could join the special set she called her "pleasure boys" without first being trained in all the Company ways and when they rose to that rank, they were individually instructed to become expert at providing whatever she desired at the moment.

All her pleasure boys were routinely castrated after they were trained to her satisfaction.

The CEO enjoyed her pleasure boys and assigned each a number that indicated how pleased she was with its performance. The newest one, #B85, was a recent boy she perfected in orgasm denial. She would have a staffer bring him to the edge – his cock hard and drooling – and then suddenly make him stop. With electricity. With ice. She repeated the process so many times that any hard cock thoughts he might have had in his former life now made him understand now that its only purpose was to get soft instantly when she demanded. Which was always. After months of training, he stiffened when he saw her and mentally commanded the cock that hung between his legs to droop like a worm. The staff nicknamed him "squishy."

She enjoyed watching #B85's face when he was called to her suite. When she finally granted him entry and he crawled toward her, his face reddened as his cock filled only with his need to obey her. And when she glanced at him, he succeeded into making it flop and hang limp between his legs. He knew what his punishment would be if he failed.

By the time he was ordered out of her office, his wilted penis was beet red from slapping or black-and-blue from beating or thick from her tablet's dark blue button that filled the implant in his shaft with saline just so she could demand that he make it soft. The clever implants made sure that was impossible.

When she announced Company-wide punishment days, they were welcomed by the staff because she was always happy when she could spend a few hours using her pleasure boys, her personal treat when punishment was completed.

After watching the video of a new boy who was branded as #B78, the CEO knew that she would not only force him to submit completely, but also make him into a replacement anal boy. After having her fill of her old anal boy, #B67, he was castrated and dispatched to a remote Company installation in the frozen north. His only job for the rest of his life was to make sure the division manager was satisfied every day in whatever manner she wanted while knowing he would never experience an erection again during his lifetime at the Company. He was forced to thank the CEO for removing only his balls; she was gracious enough to leave his cock attached but that just made his peeing on schedule work more quickly.

The CEO's punishment for violations of the no-erection policy was castration. #B67 felt the wrath of her consequences for having a stiff cock in her presence.

This new boy's egregious conduct that brought him to be assigned to full anal-boy training? When he was an international company's VP of Legal, he ran a lucrative patent trolling operation that put at least six women-led startups out of business. She could not abide his constant brief-filing and requests for continuances that drained the women's finances as they fought his baseless lawsuits.

She trained him incessantly. Nothing raised her ire like a boy who treated women badly in business.

During the first 12 months of his five-year pleasure-boy training, she had his anus expanded by #54, using one of her favorite techniques that she had taught to all her trainers. #54's expertise was in readying the staff for corporate events and this former patent troll was to become the Company's event director's assistant. He needed instruction to master the all the levels of attention to detail and working with the Company's deadlines demanded by the CEO.

Originally, he expected his new job to be a lot more than just kneeling next to the event director and taking copious notes while occasionally being required to rub her feet with his face. Over time, he learned that he could be happy only when his tongue tasted the toe of her leather boot. But the CEO knew his happiness was much more than that. Each lick was carefully learned and practiced until it was perfect. Step-by-step practice and techniques to reach the CEO's goal was what every boy learned at the Company.

Sometimes a boy with a tight ass was useful; in this case, the CEO wanted this former patent troll's ass as wide as possible. After giving out so much crap to others, he would learn what it felt like to no longer control his own shit.

A pleasure boy's training was arduous and long. Each had to not only learn techniques that pleased women in general; but was also instructed that what they used to believe about pleasing a woman was empty and incorrect. The Psych staff built a complete training program and each pleasure boy lived it for at least a year before he was allowed to satisfy a staffer.

The first task that pleasure boys learned was tongue exercises. During training, their tongues were clamped and stretched so it could provide more satisfaction to women. The boys never spent a minute without their tongues in a stretcher for the first 30 days of training. By day three, the screaming usually stopped and on day 31, when their tongues were released, the boys were so thrilled to be freed that they never complained when the same tool was applied to their penises. The CEO preferred long, soft cocks. They were easier to whip.

For the ex-patent troll, the stretcher was used on his sphincter.

Chapter 10

As the train pulled out of the station and headed north, the CEO spent the first hour of the journey reviewing trainers' notes and watching video with her top staff. The Intake team offered their final comments and shared specific observations with #34, who would bring them before the CEO. When she finalized and approved them, the training regimens were brought to the senior Trainer meeting.

Sybil's fourteen years with the company had seen her rise rapidly within Company ranks. She was exactly what the CEO wanted in human resource management – a woman who asserted the CEO's policies in every policy – and treated her underlings with iron-fisted control. #34 had been tagged with her new number after her own grueling training and she wore the #34 brand proudly above her right nipple. She longed for the day her number would inch up even higher in the Company's ranks.

The training prescribed for Sybil was exhausting and specific to the CEO's needs. She demanded that her top HR Trainer show no mercy to others yet exhibit complete submission to the Company and especially to the CEO. She displayed characteristics that the CEO wanted in a trusted head Trainer: oversized breasts, an active clitoris that produced loud orgasms when she received her annual reward, a plump ass that wanted to be filled and nipples that protruded and tightened when the wearer was called to attention.

After Training, Sybil was allotted an hour of the CEO's day for months and the 23 other hours were spent under the supervision of the retiring HR director. She endured hanging by her nipples to stretch her bosoms and learned how not to scream loudly when the CEO decided to have the director-in-training's labia pierced and installed with a director-level ring.

The CEO handled the final test herself before she would award Sybil the coveted #34 designation. Naked and ringed, she knelt on a raised platform as the CEO shut the door and turned off the cameras. Promotion tests were always private between her and her staff. She put Sybil through the required paces and then added a few new challenges of her own.

Sybil withstood the jaw spreader and nipple biters without too much reaction. A pussy spreader was attached to allow the CEO to watch Sybil's face as a thruster inserted a flexible cock into it each time the CEO pressed a button that she alone could access. While the machine repeatedly drove the cock into Sybil's pussy, the CEO sat at her desk and reviewed a few videos, read some staff notes and had tea before turning her interest back to what the cock was doing.

Sybil's face was contorted into a visage of sheer determination to not allow an orgasm that would deny her promotion on the spot. The CEO smiled and slowed the cock before eventually stopping it.

With no words of comfort or even of recognition of the torture she had just inflicted, the CEO instructed her to clamp a spreader bar to her ankles and then summarily yanked her up and hung her upside down. Using her favorite rod, she turned it on and pressed the violet light to the overused pussy. Again and again. Each time, a little zap filled the air and Sybil screamed.

When the CEO was satisfied that the heir apparent to #34's role at the Company was completely spent, she lowered her to the floor and turned away. The final test was about to begin.

Those were the only two unaccounted for hours in Sybil's personnel record. When it was over, the Esthetics Department was called to brand her new number visibly on her breast and in a hidden location that only the CEO knew. Sybil had become her new #34.

Chapter 11

Everyone in the top-level staff knew that First Training on the train trek began promptly at dawn and started in the CEO's custom car. Each Trainer appeared no later than 10 minutes before the sun rose. They had all learned never to keep their CEO waiting and at exactly 5:58, the specific rise of the sun according to the naval observatory clock, she spoke to them.

"Claim your trainee," she said. "Training begins now."

The senior staff knew that she would go over the specific training notes with them after the boys were locked in place and blind to their surroundings. New hires would wait with only one of their five senses providing any input, while she instructed her staff how to proceed with this training session's final set of plans. It was, as usual, a brilliant design and the training car was engineered specifically to reach her goals.

The first goal was always the same.

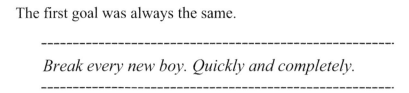

Break every new boy. Quickly and completely.

The five senior training staff members drew in a collective deep breath and walked smartly through the electronic door that wooshed open and into the adjacent car that held their charges. For their part, each of the new hires was locked in his own bare compartment and was deaf and blind to anything outside of his four walls.

Each Trainer lined up in front of her boy's cell, drew her shoulders back and waited for the CEO to order the doors unlocked. The CEO watched her trainers from her panoramic video feed and smiled at their erect posture.

Breasts out. Head straight. Chin up. Legs slightly apart. Wrists grabbed behind you. Train them with your body's stance as well with as a single word.

With a woosh, five doors opened simultaneously, and five boys stared at the woman filling his doorway.

James

James was used to sitting on the floor and this was not the first time his bare ass had been flat on concrete in a cell. Prison trained him to wait until he was told what to do next and to do nothing until he was so ordered. The CEO had selected his Trainer after consultation with the Psych Team and with her own best instincts. He was not the Company's first ex-con, but he was their first rapist and sexual batterer. She had unique training plans for the kind of man who raped and brutalized women.

He stared at the door and barely reacted when it wooshed open. But what caught his attention was who stood there. A large-breasted, full-figured woman filled the doorway. Her posture was erect, like his old prison guards. His mind filled with still-raw memories of the block commanders in prison. He knew what they were capable of doing to him; he was not sure she would be any different from them. What he knew was that he was scared to find out so he did what he had learned to do: nothing.

She stared into his black eyes and he reflexively looked toward the floor while trying to waddle his ass backward and retreat toward the small cell's wall. He felt her eyes drill into him and he lifted his knees to his chest as if to protect himself from her visual wrath. James would have curled into a ball if she had not just then given him a specific order.

"Stand!" she said in his direction but not "to" him. His body knew what to do and he rose to his feet.

What James did not realize is that his little penis and wrinkled balls were also rising to attention.

Cocks will never interfere with training. The cock is nothing more than an appendage they wear. It belongs to the Company and to the CEO.

#62 knew exactly what to do. "No," she said and pointed at the little penis that was trying to stand up.

James was shocked as she clamped a black device to the cock tip and let go of the spring to force its teeth to clamp together. His prison training was no match for her kind of authority over him and he yelled at the top of his lungs from the cutting pain that consumed his genitals. Nothing but blinding agony filled his body and he continued to screech as she turned away and unconcerned about his noise. She motioned for him to follow behind her, biting clip intact.

"I am #62," she said as James forced himself to fall in behind her. He screamed the entire walk to the CEO's training car.

Ignoring his tear-stained face, #62 tugged the clip and deposited James onto the depressed foot holes in his cubicle in the training car and locked him into place. She stood in front of him and stared into his tearful eyes while she closed the box that encompassed his head. She did not say a single word as she locked it shut and turned away.

He stood in total blackness and none of his five senses saw, heard, smelled, tasted or felt anything

Cory

Cory focused on his Trainer's long blonde hair and his eyes looked up and down her sturdy physique. He started to smile but her straight lips made him think twice, so he suppressed the grin. She did not say a word as she took two self-assured steps into his small compartment and she spoke well-trained single words.

"Up!" she said and counted silently how many seconds it took Cory to rise to his feet. Once he was in proper position, she stared at him silently until he figured out she wanted him to straighten his shoulders.

Cory remembered his first high school basketball coach who always admonished his players to stand up to their full height. His 6'4" frame still looked good, he thought, so why not capitulate to this woman's small demand? He straightened his shoulders and let his arms drop to his sides.

She pointed at the floor and still said nothing.

Cory looked at her quizzically and, in #54's opinion, took too many seconds to decipher and then obey her silent expectation. She pulled a compact wand from her belt and aimed it at his soft cock. Two clicks later, he crumpled to the cold concrete, screaming in horror at the top of his lungs.

"I am #54," she said when he stopped screaming for a moment. Cory's trek to the training car had officially begun. Her name was the only full sentence trainers were permitted to speak to new hires and only once. They had to learn to memorize important information.

Cory's tall frame was neither imposing to the staff nor was his touting of this college basketball days, medals, trophies or other sports accomplishments at all interesting. The training teams had seen boys like him before and easily broke arrogant athletes. In this case, they knew how to put a stop to his jock mentality immediately. No one at the company ever wasted time listening to boys' self-aggrandizing. They were all too busy meeting – and surpassing – their CEO's demands for the benefit of the Company.

Turning her attention to her trainee writhing on the cell floor, she used the toe of her boot to raise his chin so he could see her eyebrows dart upward. The only thing better than a one-word command was a silent one that was obeyed quickly.

In Cory's case, he was so bewildered that he did not comprehend her gesture and therefore did nothing but continue groveling and writhing, intermixed with screaming. Groveling was unacceptable behavior at the company unless the CEO required it from an employee for her particular purpose. #54 certainly wouldn't tolerate that kind of behavior from a new hire.

She pointed upward. Cory's eyes fought to focus against the bright overhead light. She waited and counted silently. His right leg moved. Too long, she thought.

Don't give them time to respond. Immediate
response is the only acceptable response.

His balls, now stained dark red from her wand's recent kiss, drooped between his legs. Red was one of #54's favorite shades for her trainees' scrotums, so she moved her boot between his thighs and lifted it up forcefully. Not quite a kick but definitely more than a simple nudge.

Cory, who had semi-composed himself only a few seconds ago, shrieked again and fell flat on the cell floor but #54 anticipated his untrained reaction and stomped her boot on his burning testicles. She smiled when she realized she caught the shriveled cock under her heel as well. It was just a small piece of the boy's shrunken cock but #54 wanted it to match the color of the squashed testicles, so she pressed her foot left and right until all his genitals were under her boot.

She pointed up again while stepping harder and ignoring his shrieks. This boy had to improve his response time so she reached into her bag of tricks and chose a well-tested cure-all for slow responses.

She waited for most of his noise to stop and then rolled him over with her foot, attached a leash behind his agonized cock and balls and lifted him by the leash, leaving no time for him to refill his lungs and start screaming again. Cory finally began to rise with only the strength of self-preservation, then to his shins and then finally to his feet. He had just become another new boy who had been trained to stand on a leash.

Males are easier to manage without verbal commands and leashes were Company policy. After training, males responded quickly to a superior's move and offered their leashed organs without the superior having to utter even a single word command.

Ignoring his tear-stained chocolate brown face, #54 tugged the leash and led Cory toward the CEO's training car. She deposited him onto the depressed foot holes in his training cubicle and locked him into place. She stood in front of him and stared into his eyes while she closed the head box. She did not say a single word as she locked it shut and walked away.

Cory's head was locked in an opaque sealed box. He heard, smelled and saw nothing but blackness. And he began to scream in a wasted effort because no one was listening.

Henry

Henry's Trainer strode into his cell and he stared at her tall boots take every step. It appeared the first time that a woman who had authority over him noticed his leather boot interest but this would be the first time a woman used it openly and to her advantage. Besides, in the past, he had to pay for the pleasure of licking boots. This promised to be better, Henry believed.

Unlike the other new hires this season, Henry did not mind his bare surroundings. Programmers are generally quiet loner types and Henry was true to the stereotype. The training he was about to begin would show him exactly how alone he could be. In short order, he would learn the only way he could be happy for the rest of his life was when he was not alone but when he was submitting to his superiors.

#71 hardly looked at him while she spoke her first single-word command.

"Stand," she said.

Henry rose sluggishly to his feet. He had not rested well on the hard floor and he was in no mood to get up quickly. She counted the seconds it took him to stand up as commanded.

"Posture!" she said when he got to his feet. Henry's shoulders inched up slightly and he sucked in his protruding gut in a futile attempt to make his out-of-shape stomach look more toned. His eyes fell to her boots again and she noted it and entered it into his training records. It was time to let him know that she owned his fetish and he would never enjoy it on her watch.

Henry was used to brown-skinned women in his department at work. IT always attracted the brainy Indian women with their clipped English sentences. Always to the point, rarely off-topic, hardly ever chatty. He disdained her at first sight as "one of them."

The toe of a polished boot crushed into his small cock and balls. Henry fell to the cold floor and a scream escaped from his throat that voiced the pain she just gifted to him. His chest heaved while he squealed like a pig in pain rolling uncontrollably in its sty.

She stepped authoritatively again and Henry did his best to look at her with contempt. She stared past him toward the bare wall behind him and visualized his skimpy body hanging from an "on call" hook with the other new hires, waiting for the CEO to require their services or a supervisor's order to start a new task. One of her favorite expressions was, "On the wall," where boys who were not needed were hung from hooks, their toes barely touching the floor.

When the CEO wanted a boy or two, she would instruct the staff to "Bring me two tight asses," or "Get me three bitches to test a boy's no-erection skill." On occasion, she would call for "a eunuch for my massage." Her top-level staff would unhook those boys that met her needs at that moment and drag them by their leashes to her presence. While she used them, the rest of the boys on the wall listened to their screams and her personally delivered punishments for any inadequacies they had the misfortune of doing while she watched.

Being "On the Wall," was the on-hold place for the Company workers.

In his cubicle and now backed into the wall, Henry trembled. #71 did not miss his fear and recognized the tell. She knew she would use it to her advantage.

"Down," she said simply. Henry stared at her with a look that seemed to demand that she repeat herself, a step #71 would never take. She drilled into his body with her eyes and let them focus on his shriveled genitals. His skin crawled under her gaze. He knew what she was looking at. How dare she?

Henry opened his mouth to complain and #71 raised one eyebrow while she continued to inspect his cock. He lowered one hand as if to hide it from her piercing gaze.

She pointed "down" with her eyes. Henry just stood there, trying to shield his cock and balls from her. He was uncomprehending, partially from confusion as well as from outright defiance. The Trainer could feel his insolence that was totally unacceptable for boys. She ran through the training steps one more time and began to execute them.

Before he could manage to focus on her movement, #71 had grabbed one testicle and yanked it down and back, pulling it up between his legs. She secured it with a tight loop and ran it around the other testicle and pulled the noose tight. Henry was afraid she was going to cut them both off if she pulled any harder.

Which is exactly what she did.

Then she attached the cock and ball noose to her knee brace and marched toward the cell's door. Henry would either fall to the floor and crawl behind her or he would become their newest company eunuch, one of several the CEO kept in their pen and used for her own esthetic desires. Her eunuchs occupied special quarters at the company and were afforded the most fashionable wardrobe to wear when serving her. Her eunuchs were the only boys allowed to wear clothes during regular company hours and only if it pleased her at that time.

#71 wondered if Henry's programming skills would suffer if he joined the eunuch class – which he would if he did not pick up the pace. Her lips turned slightly upward at the thought. The CEO did not keep every castrated boy as one of her special eunuchs unless they performed well. The unwanted ones were deposited at the nearest train station, naked and penniless, to find their own way home.

Henry's mouth spat out an occasional understandable expletive about #71's skin color, hair length and demeanor.

"I HATE you! You're SLIME!" were two of his favorite pejoratives.

Her reply was succinct. "Pcht!" It was #71's oft-used sushing term from her original language. She continued their trek toward the training car with Henry cursing and flopping behind her as the noose around his testicle tightened so much that his little balls began to turn blue.

Boys were never allowed to talk to trainers without being asked specific questions so #71 trained Henry in that lesson first. Typical red ball gags were rarely used at the company. Instead, the CEO preferred bits that forced jaws apart. With their mouths forced open, all a boy could do was drool. Grunting was also terminated by the spreader she forced between their upper and lower teeth.

It was time for Henry to learn respect for her and through her, for the entire female staff at the Company.

She swirled her long hair to a single shoulder and lifted the testicle noose and forced him to the floor and onto his back. The pain elicited an open-mouthed guttural scream, which was exactly what she wanted. The jaw spreader was locked into place before Henry realized that she had gagged his mouth wide open.

He was at a loss for words, literally and figuratively. Drool flowed onto his chin. She ordered him to stand up.

Ignoring his tear-stained face, #71 tugged the noose and led Henry into the training car. She positioned him on the depressed foot holes and locked him into place. She stood in front of him and stared into his eyes while closed the head box. She did not say a single word as she locked it shut.

Henry stood in total darkness and heard, saw, smelled, tasted and felt nothing.

Oliver

There were never enough new servers, cloud solutions or wireless devices to make Oliver happy. He did not need people around him at work; rather, he preferred an office with a door that closed and a satisfactory budget that allowed for the most cutting-edge toys and tools he could play with. At the CEO's Company that just acquired him, he was destined to learn new appreciation for the more basic mechanics of his new job.

The CEO chose #67 to train him in the way she demanded for all workers but moreover, she insisted on a special set of skills for him to master that were set out for the more promising programmers by HR staff and the Psych team. Tech workers were a different breed, the CEO knew, and tech toys and tools made them eager to get up in the morning and work hard. Because the company's technology needs were so complex and ever-changing and because warding off troublemakers before they made trouble was good business, she developed strict training for tech boys' bodies and attitudes. If pain with a purpose was good for her boys, then two distinct kinds of pain created uniquely talented IT staff.

Like most of his counterparts in the tech industry, Oliver's physical build was slight, his hair always looked uncombed, he emitted a "leave me alone" aura and usually needed a shower. All of those traits were about to be eliminated and the CEO was certain that #67's training talents would force Oliver to evolve into the kind of tech staff on whose work the Company not only flourished, but also moved forward.

Oliver was cold in his compartment when his Trainer entered with the same two step choreography that the other trainers used. He was cranky that no one had offered him coffee or even a soda and his

53

mouth was dry. His skinny body shivered when it touched the steel floor or the bare walls. There was nowhere for him to get comfortable. He missed his adjustable office chair.

He was not surprised when he saw her; network security brought him into contact with a lot of Asian women. He knew they were smart but never as well-versed in hardware or security as he was. They were good; just not as good as him.

"I'm cold," he said when she entered.

Boys are not allowed to talk to Trainers. Their job is to respond to their superiors' questions. Never engage with the new hires. Teach them the value of their silence using pain.

She stared at him and let her eyes tell him that his complaint was unacceptable. This boy needed to learn that he should never initiate conversation with a woman at the Company and to make sure he understood, she issued a single-word command to remind him just how he had been prepared on the earlier trek to the bus.

She fixed her eyes on him and let him watch her scan his body from head to toes.

Oliver's face revealed his offense at her attempt to command him to do anything. Like most new hires, #67 knew that her boy was not used to taking orders, especially from a woman superior. She knew exactly how to handle the kind of boy that showed the slightest reluctance to obey instantly. She illustrated her power quickly.

She pulled a harness over his head and stuffed a spreader between his jaws.

Oliver gurgled as she stepped back and resumed her erect posture. He whimpered and whined through the tools' straps. She pointed to his feet and ordered him silently to fall into place behind her.

"I am #67," she informed him as she glanced at her breast and remembered the day she was named.

#67's goals for Oliver's training focused on exercise, cleaning inside and out as well as appropriate socialization. It was time to get started.

Drawing her shoulders back and jutting her breasts forward, #67 took two practiced strides toward him. Her Asian skin shined under the fluorescent light that illuminated all the boys' cells. With her long hair pulled into a bun, she scanned up and down his scrawny body. At least this one did not have a pot belly.

Oliver was not a fan of her scrutiny and tried to find a place in his cell where he could evade her stare. The small cubicle, no more than 6 feet by 6 feet, gave him nowhere to hide. He wanted to curl up into a ball on the cold cell floor but he knew that Asian girls were always one notch below his intellect and skill levels, so he decided to bear her gaze and cede this particular battle. He'd win the next round.

"I do not like this," he complained.

"Shizuka!" she snarled at him.

Use the single word command and make it work. Never repeat or explain it. They will learn through pain and they will obey.

If he had his phone, Oliver would have looked up the word she just said but even he understood its meaning from the way she spat it at him. He stopped talking but his cock trembled and he reached to comfort it.

"Yameru!" she commanded. He did not need a dictionary to figure out what she meant this time, either.

The CEO had given prior consent to #67, who along with the HR and Psych teams evaluated that Oliver would need more than a single word command from time to time during First Training but she trained his Trainer to issue no more than one word at a time. She was allowed three words before getting him moving on the trek to First Training and she had already used two of her allotment.

Scanning all of her monitors with a practiced eye, #34 kept up with Oliver's behavior. She told #41 to deliver an alert to the CEO to view that cell's activities in real time and punched a reminder into her tablet to include this session in the evening's post-training video for review. She peered at the screen with growing interest. Tech boys were always unnecessarily stubborn and took a little more effort to break.

#67 closed her lips to save her third single-word command as she gripped the handle of her electronic baton. She moved behind him and pressed the rod's tip between his legs, into his scrotum and pushed hard. The HR and Psych teams predicted that Oliver would recognize that hers was no ordinary baton and would step forward, as his Trainer demanded, without having to suffer what kind of electricity was looming ominously in his future. Both teams were glued to their monitors and studied Oliver's next reaction. Both #67's possible promotion and the teams' training plan hung in the balance.

He took a shy step forward and then stood still, unsure of what to do next.

#67 had two choices: she could press her baton into him again or turn it on and make a painfully clear instruction. She did not really care what pain it caused him; rather, she wanted her team's plan to work.

Geeks and nerds, she sighed to herself.

She clicked the button halfway with her thumb and Oliver screeched like a caged chicken. But he still stood in place so #67 pressed the baton deeper into his balls with her thumb still hovering over the button. He *had* to get it by now, the secret viewers agreed to themselves. No one is *that* stupid, their training plan anticipated.

As a boy's intellect and tech skills rose, the Company staff learned that their common sense diminished. Oliver was the latest example of a new boy who really did not get it but was about to learn. They bent closer to their monitors to see the inevitable next successful training step.

She pressed the button all the way down.

He provided the unseen onlookers with a cacophony that made clear he was being tortured with exquisite pain. His throat exploded and his voice detonated in the small cell. #41 simply reported to her CEO: the boy's training had taken a step forward.

#67 eventually released the button and waited a few seconds for Oliver to cease his momentary insanity before she uttered her final single-word command.

"Aruku!" she said and pressed the baton into his ball sac again.

Although he had no idea what that word meant, Oliver crawled toward the cell door to start his trek to First Training rather than taste the evil baton again. He had no idea what lay in store for him. But what he had just experienced and the idea that moving forward could make the torture stop was merely the first step in the Company's new-hire personalized schooling. He just did not know it yet.

"Heel," she said, and Oliver groaned unintelligibly on the trek to the training car.

Ignoring his tear-stained face, #67 pressed the baton into his burning balls and pushed him toward the training car. She positioned him on the depressed foot holes and locked him into place. She stood in front of him and stared into his eyes while she closed the head box. She did not say a single word as she locked it shut.

Oliver stood in total darkness and heard, saw, smelled, tasted and felt nothing except his own drool running down his chin.

Evan

When the door slid open, Evan was ready with a list of demands that detailed his dissatisfaction with his treatment thus far. He was determined to share it with whomever walked into his cell. He was uncomfortable, cold and in disbelief at the prison-like quality of his accommodations. The CEO had expected his behavior to be no less arrogant and his Trainer had participated in several pre-hire strategy sessions and role plays using throw-away boys to formulate the most efficient training program for him.

There was a myriad of reasons that the CEO chose #36 to break Evan. Her lower number evidenced her long tenure with the Company and every day of her experience would be valuable for what they all knew would be a specialized training process. When the CEO had the numerals branded on #36's breast, she watched her pride overcome the pain that seared a lifelong commitment from the Trainer to her CEO. Her screams were music to the CEO's ears and the short ceremony was broadcast to all long-term staffers who were numbered 40 and below.

With her new name living forever just above her nipple, the newly branded Trainer cherished her #36 and her elevation into the CEO's trust circle. Her bodice hid her name from underlings. At the Company, anyone meeting an unfamiliar staffer was expected to expose her own breast from behind her training bodice to request she do the same. Any staff member with a higher number immediately sank to the floor, knelt and begged forgiveness for not recognizing her superior. For that failure, a higher-number staffer was punished and her session was enjoyed by the CEO's inner circle on Reprimand evenings. It built camaraderie among the staff to watch the lower numbers punish their underlings. It kept order in the Training ranks.

That's why her number was more important today; she was much more experienced and specially trained by her CEO through individual practice sessions using former corporate presidents and ex-business leaders who had been broken during earlier hires. Gauging from his pre-hire interviews and the secret video surveillance, the CEO knew that Evan believed he applied for a position in management but intended harm to the Company. She learned about his nefarious plan to attack several businesses that were beginning to implement her successful hiring model. What Evan did not know was that he was destined to be no more than one of her successes, but moving him where she wanted him to be would present a challenge for her team.

The CEO was up to the task.

Evan was not surprised that a tall, strong African American woman had been assigned to serve him and to respond to his grievances. Before #36 said even one word, he was barking orders and issuing complaints about his quarters, his need for coffee and his demand for proper clothing.

She looked past him toward the bare walls and then down to the cement floor. His cell was exactly like the others and she thought briefly about the disciplinary sessions they were going to have during his trek to HQ. Evan was the only person who did not realize what his fate was to be and that he would eventually submit just like all the others. To the Trainers, he was simply another sniveling new hire with a very bad attitude. One that they would fix.

Then she focused on his moving lips while ignoring his unhappy tirade.

Bend him in half with every moment. Then bend him deeper. Bend him often. Bend him completely. Bend him until he breaks.

She towered over him. Evan was used to being one of the tallest people in the boardroom yet #36 had at least three inches on him. He tried to get to the gym at least every other day but her muscles were much more developed than his own. He thought he owned admirable abs but her musculature made him look like a chair-bound hourly cubicle worker.

He finally stopping ranting and took a long look at her. Her height still surprised him but it was her physique that was more intriguing. He was sure that this good-looking girl was selected just for him. The corners of his lips turned upwards.

She saw it and did not hesitate.

"Crawl!" she said.

Evan stared at her in disbelief and countered with, "Are you speaking to ME?" It was not a question.

She pointed to the floor behind her.

Then Evan did exactly what the psychologist said he would do. He laughed. Out loud.

#36 fully expected it. It took just a few seconds, an episode that the CEO would replay later in slow motion, and she noosed Evan's cock and balls, drew them back up between his legs and into his asscheeks. Then she clamped a chain from the painfully compressed package to his neck collar. He struggled but her physical power simply overcame his little-boy efforts.

She emasculated him in less than a minute. When he looked down, he had no cock or balls. She pointed to the floor behind her again.

He had no choice. His balls and cock were gone! Overcome with fear and grief, Evan fell to his knees. He could not see or feel his cherished cock and balls that should have been dangling between his legs. Evan's identity was being reshaped by his Trainer for the new position the CEO had in mind for him, and all he could see when he looked down was a crease where his manhood used to hang. It looked a little like a hairy vagina.

The Company did not need a man with plans. The only acceptable hires would be boys who could benefit the Company's goals and growth. The rest of his life belonged to the CEO but Evan still did not realize it. But he would learn it soon.

#36 knew beforehand that this was going to be a difficult trek to First Training with this difficult boy. But the CEO chose her to break him and #36 was filled with determination to bring her CEO a broken boy that she would crack any way she wanted in her own way. #36's job hung in the balance. She could achieve the title of full-time high-level Trainer, but not until she proved herself with this very difficult First Training. Breaking Evan was that challenge, and she would march through hell to fulfill her CEO's faith in her skills. Evan was merely the boy between #36 and fulfilling her CEO's order. She had never relished breaking a boy like she did now. She licked her lips in anticipation.

The Intake and Psych teams' monitors focused on different angles of Evan's cell. The CEO's wall of video screens provided her multiple viewpoints of her Trainer and the boy. She sat back and watched Evan's initial breaking roll forward.

#36 could still feel Evan's reaction to her black skin, large breasts and toned muscles. Her rock-solid thighs were earned by an intense personal training plan and her own arduous exercise. #36's imposing biceps were huge and she often flexed them as a warning. At 6'2" of solid muscle, staff boys avoided meeting her in the hallways because she usually displayed her control over them with unforeseen cock kicks or anal penetrations because she just felt like it.

She brought two important lessons into this breaking session: First, Evan had to learn that only by obeying her quickly would he ever be successful in enhancing the Company goals, a task that was his while he was at the Company. Second, she would train him daily for the rest of his life. He would balk at the first one and he would be broken only when he accepted the second.

She bit-gagged him in seconds.

As the overseer of all First Training, #34's monitors focused on Evan's cell and she had her communications staff, led by #41, ready to report her progress to the CEO.

Evan was on his knees, outraged but finally silent. He lifted his arms in what must have been one of those male reactions to a perceived assault. While he tried to defend himself, #36 grabbed his left and right wrists, drew one in front and one behind, and locked them between his legs. With his arms secured, Evan was on his knees on the floor. He drooled from behind his jaw separator.

If he could have killed her with his eyes, his glare would have been lethal.

She looked past him. What he liked or did not like or what he wanted or needed just was not important.

Break him. That is all that matters.

With him gagged and cuffed, she pushed his head to the floor in the middle of his cell and his face pressed into the cold concrete. #36 moved toward him and positioned her body next to his. She was sure he recoiled from her gleaming black skin, rippling muscles and height that towered over him. Soundlessly, she grabbed his cock and balls in her mammoth hand and yanked him flat on the floor.

She took a handful of his thinning hair and lifted his face into her crotch.

"Smell," she demanded.

Evan was holding his breath in a useless attempt to disobey her single-word command. #36 waited because she knew he would choose to breathe sooner or later. They all did.

Evan finally drew in a deep breath that was filled with her aroma and tried to wrestle his face away from her pussy. His humiliation was so enormous that he began to feel traumatized and started to tremble. She forced him to suck in another breath full of her aroma.

The CEO gave her permission for certain exemptions from routine breaking because she knew that Evan would pose a unique challenge. #36 had already exercised one of them: she put a boy's nose outside her leather thong but within inches of her pussy. Boys were not allowed to be this close to their Trainers this soon in the First Training program, but Evan required special treatment. #36 was about to use a second rare technique authorized specially by the CEO.

She pressed her knee into his back and flattened him on his stomach. The she yanked his hips up and inserted an anal spreader and expertly parted his asscheeks. Gagged, cuffed and now splayed wide open, Evan's body was the target of the CEO's newest device that had been developed especially for new hires with overly inflated egos.

An ordinary trainee anal insertion would not achieve the results the CEO wanted for this boy. Although he had no idea that it had not been used before during First Training, he was to be the Company's test case. Their choice was a new plug that became known to upper-level company staff and Intake Teams as the "brutalizer." The staff in observation had their eyes glued to the monitors to see how this was used for the first time in a real breaking session. Back at HQ, all of the Medical and Psych Teams were glued to a monitor.

#34, in her new role as Intake supervisor, narrated the events in real time and #41 repeated her important comments to the CEO's speakers.

Pointed with an angled tip and widening toward the base, the brutalizer hid small spikes at the base that jutted out according to the settings on a custom app recently installed on #36's tablet. The spikes had settings for in-and-out movement, others just for pain jabs as well as several other custom routines guaranteed, Medical and Psych said, to break any reluctant boy. Different app settings allowed #36, so far the only Trainer permitted to use it, to spray irritating jolts of burning chemicals into the boy's rectum; to twist the plug internally so the wearer's growing dread was forced to his own asshole; to plunge in and out to make the wearer feel an impeding bowel explosion; and best of all, to press on a boy's prostate and force an erection.

That was the CEO's idea. Boys were never allowed erections at the Company and were disciplined harshly for them as soon as an errant one appeared. Evan was destined to live the rest of his life with controlled erections delivered by the brutalizer followed by public torture that was projected on high definition video by transmissions to all the branches from corporate HQ. He just did not know what kind of star he was being trained to become.

#36 pressed an orange button and a freakish growl filled Evan's small cell. One tap on the lime green button stopped the pain and Evan gasped for breath.

"Follow," she said but Evan's body lay inert and barely breathing. She tapped the dark gray button and several staffers had to remove their headsets while the spikes poked in and out of the brutalizer. Within seconds, #36 had the result she wanted and a screaming, crawling and semi-crazed former hedge fund manager crept behind her all the while squealing and yelping as he inched forward.

#34 knew she would include the entire trek in the evening's highlight video that the CEO would watch with her evening tea after a lovely dinner.

Chapter 12

The CEO's training car was skillfully designed by a team she put together that included space planners and engineers along with the Intake and Psych teams. She had worked with teams over several new-hire seasons to construct a training space that both met her current needs and was fully capable of adjusting and updating with new features that she required from time to time.

No new hire – neither boy nor Trainer – who experienced her training car ever exited that trip without having their lives changed forever.

Break them first and fast. Make them new. Then they become mine.

On a few train treks to Company headquarters, the CEO brought on potential women hires who demonstrated particular skillsets that she required. She found them through a special want ad written to produce unique women with trainer potential. All Company staff, from Medical to Psych and including potential women trainers, experienced the CEO's training car. Their sessions assessed their talents and exposed any of their limitations, in training that decided if the CEO wanted to keep them. The training car experience showed the CEO which of them might be useful and hired and which would not be useful to her and were expelled by being dropped off at the next convenient rail station. Only the best of the applicants made it all the way through the two-day trek to headquarters, where the real training began. Some showed themselves to be useless and were shipped to remote facilities for maintenance positions. But no one ever left the Company to return to their prior lives.

Those who failed during the train trek or could not meet the CEO's expectations were dismissed quickly. They were dropped off at the closest train station on the route. The women that she got rid of were provided the same light strapless wraparound sundress held closed by a single Velcro connector, the exact one that was provided before they embarked and was the only item they were allowed to bring on the train.

Unsuitable women were useless to the CEO. Her focus was fixated on first-class Trainer material. There were no second chances. No one offered any exit interview to those rejected; they were simply deposited at the station, wearing nothing but the light cotton sundress and paper sandals, with enough to pay for travel to their home cities. No one ever thought about or mentioned them again.

The CEO's training car was longer than a traditional train car. Its main feature was space that could be reshaped into open areas or divided into smaller spaces as needed. The movable walls isolated whoever she was training at the time from the intrusions of other people as well as removing any sense of time or location for the trainee. Her head Trainer used a sophisticated set of tools to alter space, add or remove equipment, and configure sessions as the CEO instructed. After the trek to the train and single-word command training, the CEO was ready to evaluate her new hires in person. She never inspected trainees until the chaff was expelled.

Her inspection of the women would take place after several First Training experiences for the five new boys. Later during the trek, she would evaluate a few women applicants but her focus right now was on the boys.

She had never failed to break any trainee and after breaking them, decided if she wanted to keep them. Women were different. She broke the women, too, and usually kept a few of them until they arrived at HQ. #34 knew that the CEO sometimes boarded a few female applicants that she was not going to keep, but she enjoyed training sessions and that was all that mattered. She had high standards for all her staff, so expelling them from the train was as easy as adding a brief unscheduled stop.

Her Intake team gathered in the observation area and the CEO signaled for her higher-level staff to enter the training car. The women ran to their places and stood on their marks. She checked their stances, evaluated their faces and nodded.

It was time for First Training. She said a single word.

"Walls."

Four walls rose electronically from the floor and created five separated spaces. A single wall dropped from the ceiling and stopped a few feet down and covered the boys' head boxes.

She said a second word. "Begin."

The women hurried to the boys' compartments and turned on a light that made their head boxes opaque to the new hires but transparent to the CEO. She reviewed their faces, nodded, and the lights clicked off to return the boys to soundless darkness.

The CEO preferred to see her new boys' bodies disconnected from their heads and especially from their faces. Her goal was to evaluate their visceral reactions and she had no use for their crying eyes or open-mouthed screams. First Training's goal was to take imperfect boys and turn them into employees that would benefit the Company. There was no training technique she eschewed; in fact, the Intake Team would take copious notes and mark the tools she used to break each new boy and then build them into new routines for next hires. She wielded the tools expertly and her teams learned something new during every training session she oversaw.

Her five new boys had been locked into position on special footprint indentations on the training platforms. They all faced forward while the opaque soundproof boxes were completely locked around their heads. They were blind except to blackness and deaf to everything except their own breathing. Small air holes prevented them from suffocating.

The Trainers secured a steel band around each one's waist. Ankle restraints prevented their legs and feet from moving even an inch. Their wrists and thumbs were locked to their waistbands.

They saw nothing. Heard nothing. Felt nothing. Tasted only their own dry mouths. Smelled how much training car air they were allowed. If any of them spoke or shrieked, no one listened to them. They were completely vulnerable to the CEO who sat in front of this season's new crop of hires and inspected them up close for the first time.

Her observation chair was a work of engineering art. She demanded of her engineers that she be able to move freely from side to side as well as move within reach of any new hire who interested her at the moment. Based on a scene from the long-ago show, *The Prisoner*, the mechanical and design teams provided her a telescoping chair that moved easily through the training car at the touch of a button. It made artistic use of gravity. The CEO insisted on a chair that enabled her to reach, touch and inspect every new hire at her whim. It was one of her most well-used training tools.

The new hires never saw the engineering accomplishment she had her team build. But they felt its effects.

The five new hires were harnessed and stood immobile as the CEO chatted with her senior staff, the only employees who were allowed in the training car during First Training inspection. She checked each one's breast for her branded name, a nomenclature system the CEO used throughout the organization. The way she set up naming reminded her of that staffer's importance to her each time she interacted with that employee. She did not share what each name meant with the staff. She shared their names only with the branders who kept the HR records up to date.

Having their names easily visible was part of her corporate strategy so she could easily determine each staff member's relationship to the rest of the staff and to her with a simple glance. Their experience and tenure were important when she needed a staff member to lead or develop a project.

The CEO demanded loyalty and performance perfection. She rewarded her staff at times but always demanded everything from them. They were thrilled to provide it.

There were some Company rules that were simply understood. Rule #1 was that no one ever left the Company. They might be transferred to other branches for a few years for specialized training, but they never wanted to leave, and they knew that venturing anywhere else was impossible. The new hires were about to learn what coming to work for the Company meant and how it would become the new normal for the rest of their lives.

She looked over the five new boys and observed their blind and deaf bodies. One trembled and two shivered. She watched their feet to see how many times they tried to lift one before they figured out that their feet were held in deep depressions and were locked down tight. She checked their fingers to see how many would flick them before they figured out that their thumbs were locked.

The Intake staff listened through headphones for the usual noises boys made but remained unheard outside of the sealed head boxes. Usually, boys shouted adamant questions that grew into pleading and eventually rose to near-hysterical screaming but the CEO could not be bothered with that clatter. Her policy about boys speaking aloud was well known.

Boys have nothing to say worth hearing. Trainees
are to be silent and perform.

"#34, attend," the CEO said as Sybil scurried to kneel next to her moveable chair.

"You brought on four new boys satisfactorily," the CEO said. Sybil's face beamed but she dared not smile. She knelt absolutely still, inhaled once and then held her breath. She waited for her CEO to complete her instructions. From her knees, Sybil was only #34 to the CEO, her number branded on her breast, and she treasured her high-level status at the Company.

"I am concerned about the fifth, the rich boy," the CEO said. "We'll see if your Intake process was up to the challenge I awarded you."

Sybil's heart pounded because the CEO had just invited her to watch the new hire First Training for the first time ever in her career. She stood quietly with her eyes closed as she felt the CEO clip nipple locks to the rings that pierced her breasts. The locks had short wires that the CEO attached to the chair's arm. The pain bit her breasts and was welcome until the CEO, done with #34 for the moment, moved to her next task and pressed a button that slid her chair horizontally toward the first new hire. Sybil stifled a shriek and jogged alongside the moving chair to which her pierced breasts were solidly attached.

#34 realized that the invitation to watch first training was the CEO's sporting event with her as the prey. Throughout the long hours of First Training, she stared at the CEO's fingers for any movement toward the chair's movement buttons. Her black boots clomped on the hard train car floor as she ran to stay up with the CEO as she moved her position from one new hire to the next.

The CEO had First Training matters to attend to and she focused completely on the work. To her, #34 was unimportant and forgotten.

She adjusted her chair centrally in front of the five new hires and studied their bodies one last time before beginning her evaluation of each and of the group as a whole. One trainee might show weaknesses but if two did, then the whole lot could be unacceptable. She began what her staff called *weeding,* her process of sorting the new hires into possible staff positions while she decided what their corporate roles would be. Few new hires ever changed departments for several years so *weeding* was a critical task.

The CEO nodded at #47 and she pressed several buttons on her control board and slid a lever from left to right. Five titanium rods rose from the floor and were positioned between each new hire's legs. They stopped at the perfect height for access to each one's cock and balls. The trainers snapped metal separators in place so the first thing the boys felt was tightening metal band that threatened to rip their genitals from their bodies. The sticks' round heads began a rhythmic pounding of five pairs of cocks and balls.

With a nod from #41, the CEO was assured that the boys' screaming had begun. She never cared to hear it.

While the new boys absorbed the reality of cock and ball beatings, the CEO began deeper evaluation into their physiques and reactivity. A boy's physical appearance was of little concern to her; instead, she was interested in what their mental reactions might be after experiencing that their current predicament was the last time they would feel their testicles or have their penises touched for the rest of their lives.

Only successful boys got to keep a testicle at the Company. The others did not need them.

Positioning her chair in front of the boy whose name used to be Oliver, she inspected his thin frame and excuse for muscles. His pot belly was a disgrace and she directed the Wellness Staff to be told to improve that failure straightaway. From her mobile chair, she circled around him, with #34's boots stomping on the train car floor to keep up with every movement. The CEO came to rest a few feet from his hairy white asscheeks.

"Disgusting," she muttered quietly. The staff recorded her comments onto Oliver's record and noted that the Estheticians would be directed to improve his appearance in a hurry.

#67, who had been assigned to be Oliver's Trainer, was beckoned to action by the CEO's wagging finger. She gripped one of his cheeks in each hand and pulled them apart. She glanced at #41 to make sure that Oliver's shouting had grown into hysterical screaming and reported this to the CEO with a nod. He was ready.

An overhead light was positioned to shine directly into Oliver's ass and provide the CEO a clear look. She knew that new hires on First Training day hardly expected this thorough an inspection. Indeed, part of First Training showed the training staff how the boys reacted to new experiences, a valuable insight for them that these experiences would become part of their daily lives.

She glanced at her monitor for a zoomed in view as #82, a petite olive-skinned Trainer whose natural talents with anal penetration were perfected at the Company, inserted tubing up Oliver's rectum and pressed the nozzle. The CEO did not bother to watch as #82 positioned it again and again and inserted more lubricant into Oliver's ass. Her eyes studied the close-up on her screen and #67 nodded again that his screaming was rising to near incoherency.

All Company employees had tool sets that had to accompany the workers everywhere they went. No boy would ever report to bathing, feeding, wellness, exercise or work without his own set of tools. They were issued on First Training Day and were their constant companions throughout their lifetime careers at the Company.

#82 moved aside so her Co-Trainer could inspect her work and when approved, she opened Oliver's tool set. The CEO enjoyed watching #94's setup of each boy's tools – seeing which tools were selected for him. First Training Day showed the CEO and her Trainers extensive information about the boys' acceptance of their new submission. A new hire's beginning to come to terms with his new life was gratifying to the CEO's training staff because it made their CEO happy with their work.

His tool set included a variety of instruments that the Psych team recommended and was issued only after the CEO's approval. Oliver's lifelong toolset consisted of several corporate-wide required devices plus custom tools chosen specifically for him. This set included flat-ended ass plugs, a graduated set of penile sounds and some items with new designs that were being tested on him. The CEO was eager to see how the new silver cock cage, tip closure and ball separator worked on his smaller-than-normal penis. Males who work in security often had to have their penile holes widened; they were often much too tight for Company needs.

During First Training, a new hire was not tested with all his tools; instead, the CEO judged each one's likely success for his new role in the Company with a few of the tools she deemed critical. Oliver, a network security engineer in his former life, had been assigned to a data entry position and would operate a dedicated terminal in a row of cubicles located in the outer ring of the headquarters tech department. The CEO was interested mainly in his chances for success in that role before she considered allowing him to work with more complex tools.

The first step on his new career was coping with #94's ass-insertion because this hire's ass was deemed overly tight by Medical and as such, would never be empty again as it was scheduled to be dilated every day.

The CEO checked her monitor as it showed #94 pressing a thin plug into the company's newest data-entry technician and watched #67 nod again. She was certain the boy was hysterical inside the head box and with that goal accomplished, she moved her attention to the next boy with #34 running as fast as she could to keep up with the sliding chair.

Ignoring #34's plight, the CEO decided to start First Training with #62's boy, known up until now as James.

Chapter 13

The first thing the CEO noticed about James was that his muscular body looked haphazard, as if he had physical strength but it was never toned or professionally trained. Because his name or history meant little to her during First Training morning, she focused on what she saw and sensed about each new boy. James interested her because he was in decent shape but had obviously never seen a personal trainer. She was always intrigued about self-starters.

His Trainer, #62, was eager to show the CEO that her recent trust in her and the promotion she received was not misplaced. #62, who met the CEO's requirements and was named as James's Trainer, was solid and sported a big belly and over-sized breasts, was assertive and earthy. She had finally found her real home with the Company after a notable tenure in education. She wanted to spend the rest of her life at the Company and tried to prove her worth every day. The CEO recalled her difficult transition from schoolteacher to Intake assistant, but she learned how to submit to her superiors well enough to have been promoted three times during the past eight years.

The CEO smiled at #62's belly fat rolls and large bosom that jiggled when she ran to fulfill a command. Big breasts were one of the CEO's favorite attributes in her females.

James learned not to scream while he was in prison. He figured out quickly that screaming achieved nothing except perhaps to entertain his superiors. In the training car, James recognized that whatever willpower he had behind bars was nothing compared to what would be required of him at his new job. Having nothing to lose, James was the only new hire not completely distraught inside his head box. So far.

Blind, deaf and for all intents mute, he stood uneasily as the CEO began her visual inspection. Her team supported her conclusion that ass insertion was not the best way to force James to submit to Company standards and processes. In fact, he had probably experienced enough penises in his ass in prison that another would not break him the way the CEO required. The Psych team also recommended that physical pain would not be their most effective First Training experience for him either. Forcing James to full submission to the CEO and to the Company would take creative psychological techniques.

To assess his flinch reaction, the CEO chose a long bamboo cane and slapped his locked penis with medium force. She was not surprised with his minimal reaction. She passed the cane to #62 who had recently received her own personal whipping instruction and knew what was expected of her with the new hire. Looking to the CEO for her cue and receiving a short finger tap on the chair's console, she swatted James's penis once.

#62 watched his body barely shudder and waited for her next cue. The CEO waited, watched, and mentally adjusted the schedule. Her finger tapped the arm of the chair and #62 delivered another stroke. She waited for the CEO to tap the arm of her chair, this time slightly harder. She caned his locked and exposed cock with more force.

For 15 minutes, the CEO adapted the schedule for James's Trainer to whack his cock intermittently. She kept changing the speed of her finger taps until #41 said into the CEO's speakers that the decibel level had risen significantly inside the boy's head box. Now that she was certain that her evaluation was correct, the CEO increased the pain level and staggered the timing until she noted from #41 that his yelling had turned into bellowing roars. She did not need to hear it to know that he was in agony.

It had not taken very long for the CEO to see through James's façade.

For James, it was not about the pain. He knew pain and could deal with it. What she knew was that not knowing when it would be inflicted was James's trigger. She found his weakness and used it – James was defeated when he could not predict what would happen or when. With his loss of control to the CEO's ever-changing penis caning timing, James was deemed ready to move on with First Training and would be made into a technical staff member serving the Wellness group. His job? James would make sure that the staff shower rooms nozzles and temperatures were working perfectly. One day, he might be permitted to install fixtures and not just repair the specialized nozzles that kept the male staff clean both outside and inside.

She instructed #82 and #94 to do James's first anal insertion but she did not bother to watch because the CEO knew what the result would be. She was not interested in his tears she did not need to hear that he was sobbing inside his head box.

Her fingers rested on the horizontal slider on her chair and she increased the speed intentionally just to make sure that #34 had to run faster to keep up or lose her nipples. The muffled scream #34 tried almost successfully to hide made the CEO smile.

Chapter 14

The CEO's chair came to rest in front of the next new boy. It was time to focus on repairing Cory's abhorrent habits and learn that her requirement that he submit to all women as his superiors was his first – and would become – his lifelong lesson at the Company. His disrespect of women was illustrated by his history of sleeping with one woman and tossing her aside for the next he could find was the first item that needed repair.

#54, Cory's Trainer, was chosen by the CEO for her ivory skin, long blonde hair and naturally golden pussy hair that Esthetics highlighted just for this training experience. She was exactly the kind of woman he always sought for one-time hookups. He had interacted with #54 for a few minutes before she tased his cock and balls and led him shrieking to the training car. But the CEO was not sure if he would remember at all what she looked like after that introduction.

When she arrived to review this new hire, she eyed his tall frame and, with #34, her breasts still clamped and running alongside her floating chair, the CEO circled his dark mocha body. Psych studied his arrogant attitude that permeated his interviews and even more so via their hidden camera footage. One team member pointed out to the CEO that even ordered coffee with an arrogant lilt in his voice. #54 was certain he would be more respectful after training.

They always were.

What the CEO needed was a new worker in her HR department who could score batteries of tests that would assist in their placement in the company. Cory, an HR professional in his life prior to accepting the offer with the Company, would have to be trained first to submit to the same type of woman he used to abuse emotionally and then to the layers of female staff and supervisors he was going to answer to. Finally, he needed training in administering the Company's specialized tests and in learning how to work quickly and accurately.

Adapting to the Company way was a brutal learning experience and Cory was going to be trained to help make new male hires ready for their own brutalization. During his new career, his athletic frame would come to love the taste of his superiors' boots. Any thoughts or longing he had for their bodies would become a long-forgotten memory.

With his tall body at her fingertips and his head neatly packaged in a sensory deprivation box, the CEO glanced at #34, still chained to her gliding chair. She had shed no tears yet. But she would eventually. They always did.

Everyone in the training car noted the longish cock and Cory's densely hairy pubis. They all knew at least one of them would disappear soon – the hair or the cock- and wondered if he would be one of the few that the CEO would take for her own personal boy after removing his genitals. Would he be the boy in this crop that she converted into her own eunuch? Or would he lose a single testicle like all the others and become just another worker at the Company? Her manicured fingers reached out and yanked a handful of public hair. #41 confirmed a small yelp was emitted inside the box.

#47 tapped tablet and Cory's legs moved apart. His long cock hung straight down. She eyed her training staff and #88 stepped forward, her tools of her trade neatly boxed in a clear kit. She opened all four sides to reveal the CEO's plan quickly to change this boy's attitude toward Company women.

With his feet locked, #47 raised Cory's platform and his tall body was stretched full length. His splayed legs remained solidly in place and his cock and balls were fully available as #88's target. She applied hot wax to the entire pubic area without first trimming his curls. With each pad that she pressed into the wax and tore off, it yanked huge tufts off his genitals. With his dark pubic hair and skin as her palette, the boy's cock area began to shine in a bright circle.

She glanced at #41 who nodded again. Yelps had turned into guttural screams. Satisfied, the CEO had #88 continue to create a widening circle of hairless nakedness that surrounded a set of balls and a cock that hung limply, devoid of its usual excitement.

Inside the box, Cory was in the middle of a rising panic attack. The pain was almost unbearable as each application of hot wax ripped off more of what felt like his own skin being torn away. As #88 worked, she stripped hair from each testicle, squeezing each one agonizingly tightly in her fist, stretching it out and inspecting it with a forehead magnifying light. All Cory felt was different kinds of rising brutality in rapid succession. Fear derived from not knowing what was terrorizing his prized cock grew inside him as he suffered through #88's vicious work.

Finally, she took the tip of his cock and pulled it straight down. A few hairs lingered.

With her magnifying light peering onto Cory's dark cock skin, she used medical tweezers and yanked out each follicle one by one.

#41 was sure everyone in the training car could hear his pathetic screams but the soundproofing was denser than his lungs could pierce. With a tap on her armrest, the CEO started the motor to lift his legs from the training pad and raise them toward his wrists. Within moments, the new boy's ankles were secured to his wrist restraints and his spread legs revealed a fully open ass with naturally spread asscheeks.

His hairy ass was #88's new target.

Hot wax applications generated louder screams inside the box and her ruthless removal techniques exacerbated Cory's full-out sobbing. While the CEO and her staff remained oblivious to Cory's state of total panic, #88 cleaned every hair from inside his ass crack before peering inside to check for any remaining hairs. Each one she found was removed with her tweezer expertise.

She inspected him one last time before kneeling before her CEO.

"Well done," she remarked as the esthetician prostrated herself in gratefulness and returned to her place among the Trainers.

Dangling like a side of beef in a meat warehouse, Cory's ass was resplendent in its bald glory. Still hanging with his ankles and wrists sharing a single lock, the boy was sobbing uncontrollably and shrieking his grief to an unhearing and uncaring audience. His first lesson in his Trainer using pain wisely was finished and the next training steps they used would capitalize on what they learned from the prior torture they had just witnessed.

The CEO's fingers reached for the horizontal slider on her chair and she increased the speed even more to make sure that her #34 had to trot faster to keep up so as not have her nipples ripped off. The muffled scream #34 tried less successfully to hide made the CEO smile.

Chapter 15

Every online step that the Company took was well researched and carefully planned. The CEO's need for web developers who were expert at both code and design was growing and a boy with Henry's skillset was a decent new hire profile. He was arrogant, a trait the CEO could break in any new boy, and he had fair technical skills. She could use him.

Males who wrote code in their daily jobs were useful to the Company to keep the online presence and internal Company documentation up to date. Moreover, the CEO was very often an early adopter of internal communication tools and needed staff that could meet that challenge.

She enjoyed reading job applications from coders and watching their daily lives through the hidden cameras her staff set up. There was something about the clarity of thought that came from coding – having to be brief and concise – that made them easily distinguishable from other applicants based on their written answers on Company forms as well as their verbal interactions that she observed surreptitiously.

She figured Henry out after just one work snippet.

The staff set out an ambitious employment goal for Henry: he would be locked to a red bench in an open area in the center of several female superiors from whom he would be forced to take orders regularly. The staff knew that both web developers and coders were notoriously independent and pushed the edge of many envelopes until those boys were reined in tightly. Expectations had to be set and severe punishments required if any male hire violated a single rule.

The CEO expressed a desire for Henry to be trained quickly and put to useful work as soon as possible.

What was left unsaid to the training staff was that if Henry's fast-track training failed, the team that designed it would be put on the wall and used as guinea pigs for work on training procedures. The CEO regularly showed staff punishment to the entire staff in after-dinner video; it kept them all in line. Henry's trainers were walking a fine line and any failure with their fast-track training recommendations would result in a dreaded on-the-wall experience.

The CEO frequently put her staff on her wall to be used for various training tests and as vivid examples to the rest of the Company workers. Staffers who were instructed to get on the wall crawled in dread to the nearest hook and pressed their backsides into the depression. Upper-level staffers locked a metal band under their shoulders and around their upper torsos and raised the miscreant to a height that was three inches taller than their dangling toes. The wall hangers just hung in place and waited until they were useful to the CEO.

Being assigned to hang on the wall was the first level of staff punishment. Their shame was visible to everyone who walked by. Humiliation was the CEO's most feared and effective tool.

She used some the wall hangers to demonstrate new techniques or to test new training tools. Using wall hangers was how they perfected the newest anal plug that spurted burning chemicals and the scalp brander that burned their numbers on staff after hair removal. Calling for one wall hanger after another, the CEO could watch her engineers and staff go through the plug's trials that new hardware demands.

The CEO scheduled Company-wide training sessions and every staffer knew that her training test subjects were usually staffers, just like them, who needed retraining or who had earned special punishments. Just a few months ago, a Trainer who mis-entered a step into the online manual was hung by her heels along with her entire team, and #72 whipped each ass until they were all welted with glowing black and blue marks that resembled the company logo. The

CEO made sure that video was played every day for a week after dinner for the full staff.

Lessons are learned from pain, and fear and the humiliation that you may be next.

After the staff witnessed punishment and saw how retraining was done, when the CEO gave staff orders, they obeyed her instantly and without question. And so it would be with Henry's special training.

Although he seemed to know his way around code and had written several insightful routines that, with a few modifications, the Company could benefit from, Henry's everyday vocabulary at work denigrated every woman with whom he interacted. The CEO would have both: an excellent coder and an employee who knew his place with women staffers, all of whom would be his superiors for the rest of his life. Or she would have neither and Henry would become another castrated staff member who picked up trash or sorted recyclables.

She assigned #71 for Henry's First Training because she had honed a set of skills that had successfully broken a few hires who were just like him. Her brown skin, long black hair and strict Indian upbringing coalesced to foster her orderly training and adherence to the CEO's plan. With her ability to follow the Company plan in every detail, #71 was one of her most competent Trainers.

It was company policy never to change thinking. Destroy what they believe. Then build attitudes that the Company demands.

Henry was used to issuing orders and arguing that his staff and co-workers did not carry them out successfully or the way he had in mind. What they learned from interviews replete with hidden cameras was that he withheld crucial information just so he could berate the design staff, especially female workers, alter goals and make sure they could never meet his ever-changing expectations. Destroying that was the first goal of Henry's fast-track training.

With all his senses except feeling what touched his skin taken away, his scrawny body trembled when #71 pressed her fingers into his ass. He tried uselessly to bend forward apparently trying to protect himself from the intrusion when she pulled his cock forward fiercely. He shook violently when she added clips that bit into his nipples. With each new attack, Henry's body quaked.

He did not know what was coming next – or where – he would be violated.

The staff agreed that unnerving this boy was a first step in building a useful coder for their online needs. #71 never focused on a single intrusion; rather, she inflicted one after another to make the boy understand that whatever was perpetrated on him was simply his to accept. The sooner he learned it, the better worker he would be for the Company.

#71 followed the training procedure set by the staff and approved by the CEO. In rapid succession, she cut off his air until his entire body spasmed in a hopeless struggle to breathe, then hung weights from each testicle and whipped them in a staccato rhythm, sprayed hot oil into his ass and drove a titanium sound into his pee hole. There was no need, but #41 confirmed it anyway: the new hire was screaming so violently that he was close to a physical or psychological breakdown.

The CEO evaluated that he was now ready to undergo rapid training.

All they had to do going forward was to remind him that he would do whatever he was instructed, or he would be punished severely, immediately and unexpectedly. Prior new boys spent years trembling and flinching when they walked to or from feeding or bathroom time, terrified that a Trainer would look at him closely.

Her fingers reached for the horizontal slider on her chair and the CEO moved the speed lever to an even faster setting and watched #34 all-out sprint in fear of losing her nipples. #34 no longer tried to hide her screams of pain, a sound that made the CEO smile.

Chapter 16

His balls still screamed from the torture #67 inflicted on them minutes before in his cubicle as Oliver remained senseless in the headbox on the training platform. He longed to caress his balls and tried to remind himself that they were *his* cock and balls. The tech boy training procedure that was perfected by the staff on prior hires like him would prove him wrong. That process always did.

#67 stood in front of her boy and waited for her CEO's signal to begin. The CEO appreciated certain very useful staff members and often rewarded them for their successes in front of the larger workforce.

She praised her women's successes, highlighted their triumphs, and grew their loyalty and submission with every word she spoke.

When the Company hired two new tech boys several seasons ago, #67 was selected to try out a new multi-boy training regimen. She was named #84 before that experience and the CEO had already been considering elevating her rank for several good years of service. Right now, it all depended on her success with the new two-boy program.

The HR staff studied a new technique for two-boy intakes with the approval of the CEO. Their plans were a little edgy and had not been tested yet, even with full-time staffers. They designed a trial scenario to illustrate their plan.

The CEO ordered a few tech boys to be hung on the wall so she had enough to use and discard as the teams and #84 progressed through the practice sessions. She had the first two boys delivered and ordered them hung alternately up and down by their steel chest and hip bands so that each one's face pressed into the other boy's genitals. Using noise-canceling headphones and opaque eye masks, each boy had only his face, lips, tongue, and teeth to explore the warm flesh against which his face was secured.

What made the experiment unique was that the boys' mouths were not gagged, and the assessment team could hear everything they said. Or cried.

The first set of boys experimented with were two of her long-term submissives and each unabashedly explored the other's sex. A few face rubs, a bit of tongue washing, some non-aggressive tonguing. Not at all what the team wanted or expected. She discarded those two and had two more tech boys taken off the wall but this time they were locked onto portable platforms with one on his stomach and the other atop and in the other direction. Bottom boy's ass was lubricated with mild *fire* gel. Their waists were clamped together and the only movement top boy could make was to hump his hips.

The CEO watched the trial unfold. With a few humps started by #84 swatting top-boy's ass, top boy figured out what was being demanded of him and pressed the tip of his flaccid cock toward bottom boy's ass. His squealing, broadcast for all the trainers to enjoy, delighted the staff, who enjoyed the trial of a new program that was playing out in real time in front of them.

The CEO leaned in and top boy did not disappoint the teams' predictions. With soon-to-be-renamed #67's expert use of the Company electronics, she raised bottom boy's metal waist band and lowered top boy. The boys were splashing and slapping against each other's sweat – with top boy piercing bottom boy and bottom boy's ass raising up to meet his hardening cock.

The CEO recognized the success of the trial and the Training staff knelt in front of her to be recognized for their success. She had top and bottom boy put back on the wall before any pesky orgasm threatened strict Company policy. She then addressed the staff.

"My boys never get hard," she said as the training staff's faces melted in dejection. They knew that punishment awaited them.

The CEO meted out punishment immediately. That evening, the training staff and still-named #84 were hung from chest and hip bands and pressed into each other in a circle where each's face was forced into the other's ass so tightly that they all struggled to breathe unfettered air. As she broadcast their punishment company-wide, every staffer was reminded that no matter how high up you were in the corporate structure, you must obey every order and when you fail, you submit to punishments even if that involves cleaning your co-workers' asses with your tongues a few hours after their dinners had been laced with a fast-acting stool softener.

#84 put in extra hours, submitted to retraining and began another two-year climb before she was awarded the coveted #67.

Today was the newly-minted #67's first chance since that trial to regain the CEO's favor and begin trying to climb further up the Company ladder. She reviewed every training manual and requested extra personal tutoring from the overseer that #34 selected. After surviving the Company's leadership training a second time, #67 was eager to display her new talents in Oliver's first training. She had a lot to prove.

#67 worked for years to perfect tech boy training along with the humiliated members of the training staff. They used several sets of boys on the wall, using and discarding one set after another as they worked through their new two-boy program. It was time to demonstrate how quickly she could train the new hire.

His head surrounded by soundless blackness, Oliver had only one vision: a Japanese woman detonating pain into his balls. He hated that – and he hated her – and knew that she would make a mistake that he could capitalize on. Oliver knew that women always erred. He just had to wait for it and use it to his advantage.

Her interaction was being watched closely by the staff in the training car and evaluated by the CEO. #67 felt ready for the challenge. Her first step was to remind the boy that testicles no longer belonged to him but were Company property when he was hired and for the rest of his life. She jabbed the baton into both dangling balls and discharged it once. #41 confirmed the decibel level of Oliver's first shriek.

#67 motioned for a boy she had on the wall and had him dragged to the training platform. He was outfitted in the staff's new training tool: a solid ball pouch with a thick semi-flexible penis sticking straight out. Sporting a portable headbox, the boy stood on a platform that was raised until his artificial cock reached Oliver's asshole and his hands were locked to the boy's chest band. #67 pressed the cock into the hole and pushed a button to start it. Electronics took over and the recent wall-hanger began fake-fucking the new hire. It was then that he understood he was merely a tool and would feel nothing. Every boy on the CEO's wall was for her use and, each learned it more deeply every day.

Oliver, on the other hand, believed he was being fucked in the ass by an unknown male and struggled uselessly against the unyielding metal bands to escape the violation. The only part of his body that moved at all was his little cock. #67 immediately pressed her baton into it and discharged it on a medium setting.

#41 confirmed that Oliver was hysterical inside his head box.

The CEO leaned in and every Trainer noticed her interest. In under two minutes, #67 had taken a new tech boy and turned him into a hysterical mass of quivering, screaming flesh.

#67 watched her CEO for a sign. When she nodded, #67 fell to her knees in gratitude as Oliver continued to be fucked by an anonymous boy's fake cock and would continue to be used until the CEO's fingers reached for the horizontal slider on her chair and moved the speed lever to yet a faster setting. Everyone watched #34 break into a full-out sprint while screaming at the top of her lungs. She no longer tried to hide her screams of pain, a series of squawks and cries that made the CEO smile.

Chapter 17

The sensory deprivation box covering his head both intrigued and terrified Evan. Alone and without his entourage's familiar faces, he explored his lack of smell, taste, sight and hearing before a sense of claustrophobia began creeping over him.

The CEO had not shared her discovery of Evan's fear of closed spaces with the training staff or even with #36, Evan's Trainer. She wanted to see how the powerful dark-skinned Trainer would enhance her plans once she realized his weakness for herself.

Look for a weakness. Exploit it. Use it. Own it.

Evan was not a typical new hire for the Company and the CEO wanted his intake and First Training to be used as a recipe for future hires of his ilk. Arrogant and egotistical, Evan's training was designed specially to be brutal, quick and effective. There were no breaks built into his First Training during this trek to HQ.

When the CEO's chair touched down in front of Evan's platform, she did a quick once-over of his body to look for quivering or sweat. There was little evidence of either. She had #82 and #94 on hand to assist #36 in this inspection. None of the Trainers knew exactly what she had planned, so they brought all their tools to be ready for almost anything.

The first step was #36's command to #94 to raise the floor under Evan's feet and make sure the tip of the electrical tool was ready to be used in Evan's ass. At the same time, she ordered #82 to insert a tube into his rectum and discharge a newly developed greenish goo into him. It was then that #41 reported to the CEO via her tablet that he was whimpering inside his sensory-deprivation box. Like the rest of the training staff, she had no idea what the green goo was doing to Evan inside the boy's rectum but the CEO's face indicated that it appeared to be doing exactly what it was designed to do.

His Trainer's muscular physique was at full attention as she drew a new tool from her belt. The training staff looked at it almost jealously; everyone wanted to be the first to try a new tool that the engineers developed. #36 fondled it lovingly a few times before tapping it lightly to one of his nipples.

The CEO's tablet glowed with #41's message: "He's screaming his lungs out."

The CEO nodded to #36 and she pressed the tool against his other nipple. When she removed it a few seconds later, the entire training staff realized what it had just done.

The boy's nipples were pierced and metal loops had been inserted. His chest was red, his nipples were beginning to swell and #94 pressed cold packs against them. No one in training had ever seen the CEO pierce a new hire during First Training and they oooh'ed at the results.

#41 was told to broadcast the result to the entire training car:

"Gasping. Panting. Intermittent screams. Decibel level high."

The CEO's strategy matched her expectations. There was only one more step to ensure the boy understood he was completely owned by the Company and would follow orders from #36, whose authority came directly from the head Trainer, who answered directly to the CEO.

It would not be complete unless Evan experienced quick total submission. One more step would ensure it. That would be a new and drastic technique. Before his first visit to Esthetics to have his body hair removed, a gift that had to be earned by scrupulously-trained and well-behaving new hires, #36 pulled yet another new tool from her vest and motioned to have Evan's leg harnesses spread so his ass was completely open to the CEO's vantage.

She noted he was puny – not much to see, just a short cock and hairy little balls – but that was not her focus. She wanted to see the new tool in action. #36 clamped the new tool to the short skin between his ass and ball sac and with a click of a single button, she pierced his frenum and installed a metal ring. #41 was again told to broadcast it.

"Full-out screaming. Mouth gasping, sucking air. Decibel level approaching 110. Heart rate steady and…"

Before she could finish, the training staff watched the snotty venture capitalist shit explosively and spurt pee from his little cock. The staff nodded, knowing this level of debasement doesn't happen often during First Training. They "ooohed" again at the CEO's strategy and #36's skill in breaking a boy like that so fast.

The CEO nodded and #36 fell to her knees in gratitude.

Inside Evan's black box, he lost control of everything: he shit in public, peed over his belly and legs, screamed into breathlessness, fought against horrific pain and was hung with his cock and balls spread for everyone – whoever was there – to see. He had nothing left. Evan broke into tears. It wouldn't be the only time that happened during his career at the company. And that would be the rest of his life.

The CEO's fingers fondled the horizontal slider on her chair and moved the lever to the fastest setting and watched #34 all-out gallop in fear of losing her nipples. #34 no longer tried to hide her screams, sounds that made the CEO smile again.

Now that the new hires were initially broken, the rest of the train trek would teach them that they would perform the behavior that the Company demanded. For now, they were left on their platforms, heads hidden within sensory-deprivation boxes, as the Trainers were released to explore their bodies, inside and out, by touching, pinching and slapping any part that interested them. They were the lower-level

Trainers who brought these five new hires to First Training, so they needed to become familiar with the boys' reactions to new sensations.

The CEO released #34 from her nipple hooks and watched her crumble to the floor in exhaustion before she zapped #34's nipples with an electrical prod to force the woman to her knees so she could properly thank the CEO for the gift she gave her that morning.

Chapter 18

The first full day on the trek toward the Company's headquarters ushered in an intense night of training that was inflicted on new hires. It came right after their first breaking session and was officially named First Training. The new boys had to learn what their new lives held in store: that their five-year commitment was really a lifetime tenure in which they were suddenly subject to all Company rules. There were no exceptions. First Night was the time that the training staff would introduce them to the Company way of naming staffers.

They were about to learn that every moment of their lives was to be in service to the Company and the CEO. Her trainers excelled at their own obedience, practiced complete submission to their CEO and earned their status to train new boys.

It was time to start their natural evolution into Company slaves.

Without warning, the five trainers stepped into the boys' sparse compartments to begin First Night work. What they saw in each cell, was a naked boy rolled into a ball on the cold floor. None were complaining of being mistreated or being kept naked or of full-body soreness. They were struggling to collect what was left of their wits after each was broken in another successful First Training Day.

In the CEO's private car, the heads of Training and Intake were meeting to finalize their nominations for the new boys' new names. After First Training Day, the highest-level staff was required to provide suggested names for their boys after consulting with the Psych and Intake teams. Names became the workers' designations for the rest of their lives. The CEO would review them and make the new names official. Once they arrived at HQ, she would brand her new boy staff with their designations.

The naming system for Company boys was complicated but clear. It drew on experiences with the boys' pasts, their assigned employment sectors and each one's potential to serve. Most of all, the naming system included important numbers. A boy with a "2" prefix was going to facilities, but the last three digits of his name signified his training potential, current status, ongoing needs and his difficulty level. Although all four digits were important, the CEO focused on how the trainers evaluated the first and last numbers for each boy.

Nothing mattered more than potential and difficulty. The chart was as complicated as it was clear.

Company Name Matrix		
1	**2**	**3**
Frequent beating *Intake Trainee*	**Stubborn** *Facilities*	**Training Check** *Web Services*
4	**5**	**6**
Malingerer *Esthetics Training*	**False pleasing** *Psych*	**Punish daily** *Technology*
7	**8**	**9**
Supervise closely *Human Relations*	**Cock amputation** *Eunuchs*	**Disrespects Women** *Special*
0	**Penis Denial**	All male staff

As the head trainers gathered at the low conference table that the CEO had positioned so they were forced to their knees, number cards were sorted and re-sorted as they evaluated the new hires. James's Intake Trainer, #55, knew he was going to Facilities, so the #2 was appropriate for his first digit. Facilities, with its plumbing, HVAC and related maintenance sectors always drew the lowest prefix. She stared at the two cards in her hands.

"Does he seem like a two or a seven?" she asked.

The other Intake trainers stared at her cards and replayed video inside their heads to help #55 make her crucial decision.

"Not sure," one said. "Is he more #2, stubborn like an ass, or more like a #7 that needs daily supervision?"

#55 thought it over for a while and then beckoned #62, James's First Day Trainer, to the table. She stood perfectly straight with her rolls of fat pleating over her big belly. Like all lower-level trainers, #62 was always naked in meetings and all-trainer events. Low-level trainers wore their leathers only when working with boys. James was a simple human being with no airs and a personality that suffered from both bad luck and his own stupidity. He was a mirror image of most men.

#62 stood silently and waited for her superior to speak.

"What do you think," she said, "would you second-digit him a #2 or #7?" She searched the Trainer's face for a clue

Like the other low-level Trainers, #62 had been schooled in all aspects of First Night and the naming ceremony and understood the designations. But offering her input on such an important process made her tense and she shifted her left foot. Every Head Trainer at the table saw it and now they knew her tell.

Before she could utter the #2 that was on the tip of her tongue, #33 pressed her prod into the fat woman's vagina, flicked the red button and shot its beam once. No one "shuffles" in front of Head Trainers, she just learned up close and very personally. It was unacceptable behavior and needed on-the-spot correction.

"Thank you," #62 managed to whisper through gritted teeth. She did not speak another word because nothing she could say was needed. Correcting unacceptable behavior by a superior immediately was how the Company worked.

"Reply," said #55 using a one-word command that kneeling trainers recognized as her exercising her total authority over the lower-level one.

"2," she said because no explanation was needed. #55 pointed toward where the other Daily Trainers were gathered in their gated pen until they were summoned by the Head Trainers.

As she crept back to the Daily Trainer pen, #62 tried to keep her head high yet knew she had been corrected during First Night and everyone saw it. She vowed silently to improve her performance every moment of every day she was allowed to work for the Company.

James would now be known only as #2-273, a facilities boy who is stubborn, needs close supervision and whose training needs to be checked multiple times throughout the day by every woman staffer he encounters. It would take effect as soon as the CEO ratified it and branded onto him once they reached HQ. They moved on to rename Henry, destined for the Web Services sector and his prefix had to be #3. It was time to build the rest of his forever name.

Breaking Henry of his misogynistic behaviors was on #46's mind as she shuffled the cards. As a #3, he would interact mostly with male web devs but would report daily to his superiors throughout his workday. Breaking his tendency to overly focus his attention, the way web geeks tend to concentrate solely on their work, was going to frustrate him every day. His trainers would interrupt him continuously on a schedule that built an environment in which he would be constantly exasperated and irritated. It was part of his learning how to appreciate his superiors' commands and obey them instantly without complaint or question.

"I'm not sure. I know he's a #4 but he's so much of a #9 that it almost overshadows it. Would you name him #4 or #9?" she asked the other Head Trainers at the table. They studied the chart, talked about his Intake and trek to the train and decided to get the input of his daily Trainer. They beckoned #71 to the Head Trainers' table.

Her naked brown skin shined in the glare of overhead lights and her long dark hair hung behind her shoulders. Long-haired girls were required to expose their breasts when their hair was down. In #71's case, her smallish bosom was almost hidden by huge dark areola from which almost-black nipples protruded. The train's temperature was always intentionally cool.

"Well?" #46 said and #71 knew she had to give an answer. The right answer. And she had only one chance to get it right.

Her mouth was dry and #71 fought to speak without licking her lips. She knew that his final digit had to be a 9 but his potential – what she should know clearly from First Day – was a tossup between a 1 and an 8. Although she did not have as much experience as #46 at the Company, #71 felt that cock removal was the only clear path for Henry. He'd never respect his superiors while that cock hung between his legs. At the Company, castration was used whenever necessary but always put a boy out of action from his work for a day or two. She said, "#1."

The Head Trainers looked at each other in surprise. They wouldn't have chosen #1 for Henry because disrespecting women, name class #9, was the ultimate failure in a man. Beating them did not assure the Company that his egregious behavior would be cured. Neither was a subordinate Trainer contradicting her superior, even unknowingly.

Without glancing at #71, #46 said quietly, "He will be #3-729. The other Head Trainers nodded at her choice. They all recognized that Henry had potential if he were supervised closely and his abysmal disrespect of women were erased. The 2 in the middle? He was stubborn and the training that would accompany the numbers 7 and 9 of his new designation would take care of that.

Then she turned her attention to #71.

"Submit to further training with Psych," she said. The trainer's dark nipples trembling with fear, #71 crept back to the trainer pen. Once there, she mouthed, "Psych" at the other trainers who winced with her. No one wanted to endure another round of Psych training. If a trainer made it through Psych, she would climb the Company ladder but those who did not complete it successfully were dropped off mostly naked at the closest train station that the CEO's train could pull into. They were never heard from or mentioned again.

Both Cory and Oliver were foregone conclusions for naming. After a bit of card shuffling, First Trainer input and several exchanged glances, Cory was renamed #7-650 and Oliver was to be known as #6-437. The Head Trainers agreed that Cory would likely be trained best if his lifelong routine included constant orgasm denial, required for all males, and they agreed for Oliver, he needed to be kept under constant supervision and be forced to answer for every action he took.

Then the group took a collective deep breath and began deciding on their recommendation for Evan's new name. Cards were shuffled and reshuffled on the low table and the women slid them around, shook their heads and slid them again. No combination seemed to fit Evan perfectly and the Head Trainers knew that their CEO would be paying special attention to this selection. They had all received the kudos for naming previous new boys and that helped elevate them to Head Trainer status. They all loved their positions in the Company. But a bad choice for this boy? They cringed when they thought of the ways their CEO might display her disagreement. And worse, her disappointment.

Using selector #9 was a rarity at the Company. Very few boys were hired who fit into this Company business sector and only a handful were allowed to stay. The unsuccessful boys were shipped off to several low-level Company branches and their lifetime jobs included cleaning, leaf raking, snow shoveling and food preparation. Although important to the Company, these jobs filled the lifetimes of those who did not respond as the CEO demanded to their training well enough to provide what the Company needed at a useful level.

There was complete agreement that Evan belonged in Sector #9. Once trained, #43 believed he could possibly bring positive results to the sector and perform duties that led to market gains. But if he failed at the training she and #36 outlined and later inflicted, he would be tossed aside like food scraps into the peat moss garden and never heard from again.

She knew that his daily trainer was named a lower number than her own and #43 was counting on Evan's training success to help elevate her own rank. But more importantly, she had been granted the most difficult new boy and the most experienced daily trainer. With new Psych techniques afforded her, #43 knew that failure would result in her own demotion and having seen a downgrading ceremony, she had no desire to participate in her own. For years, no one at the Company could tell the difference between that demoted trainer and the food slop in the scrap pile as she stood in the debris and led her workers in a constant struggle to scrape, clean and toss garbage for the entire Company staff.

The CEO took staff naming very seriously and held her workforce fully accountable.

The Head Trainers finished their naming, signed the list with their numbers and handed it to the daily trainers. The dailies entered the information into Company records and followed the Head Trainers to the Esthetics area of the train where the Heads received welcome massages to help them relax after their arduous work and the dailies were inspected for errant hairs that were to be waxed or plucked off so they were picture perfect to meet with the CEO for the Naming Ceremony finale.

Chapter 19

The CEO was poured a fresh drink and she shooed away the staff that was hovering around her. She chose her personal staff carefully and saw to it that they receive specialized training from Psych, Esthetics and Nutrition. What she required was good-tasting meals that were well-served by staff that was well-groomed and efficient. Every staffer was inspected before every interaction with her by #34 as part of her senior-level duties. It did not matter that #34 had spent First Day running to keep up with the CEO's gliding chair that had her nipple rings locked to it. She remembered every step as the chair darted left, right, up and down. No one cared if her nipples were stretched or even bleeding. Their focus was always on the CEO.

She nodded and the Head Trainers were led in and knelt in front of her in every staff member's usual position when interacting with the CEO. Each held a large card and the CEO surveyed their name nominations. She read them one at a time, left to right; paused, and then read them again. She fixed her eyes briefly to match the face of the new hire that hung at the bottom of the card to the new name proposed by her staff.

Because her staff was so well trained, she rarely disagreed with the gist of their name nominations; however, there were times that she was surprised that her females were off the mark in this evaluation. It almost startled her from time to time when five Head Trainers could be so mistaken about who a boy was and what they had to train out of him so he would succeed and benefit the company. She hoped this was not one of those days.

She started with James; she thought he was the easiest to evaluate.

"#2-273," she said almost as a question. #55 lifted her chin to look at her CEO in one of the rare times she was allowed eye contact. But she knew better to say anything unless a direct question was asked.

"I see you consider him in need of regular training, re-checking and close supervision. I agree." #55 allowed herself to breathe. "You realize that you are missing an important aspect of that boy's situation."

#55 held her breath. So did the other Head Trainers.

The CEO continued and disregarded the nipples that jiggled from the trainers' trembling breasts. "You ignored that he has been in prison. Regulated. Overseen. Closely supervised. Abused. Raped." She said each word carefully and the Head Trainers could hear the periods after each word. She went on, "You are wrong: he's not stubborn. Tell me what he is."

The direct order hung in the air as #55 struggled to see what she missed that her CEO had realized. No words were in her head. She forced her lips to open and a word fell from them. "Five?" she half stated and half asked.

"It's about time," the CEO replied and then showed the Trainer what she missed. "He is false. His entire being is fake. He performs as you expect but not with his soul." She paused before adding, "Psych knew that. I knew that. But you did not."

Hanging her head in shame at her failure, #55 realized that when they arrived at HQ, she would be assigned additional Psych training to correct her mistakes. Her soul shuddered in dread.

The CEO checked the remaining cards and nodded slightly at each. She was pleased to see her girls get the next three boys named correctly but she was particularly interested to see what they came up with for Evan. She knew they spent most of their time during Naming figuring out what new name captured this particular boy the best.

She studied #43's face and noticed an anxious tic. Her tell, those little facial twitches, were sure signs of her self-doubt. "You're certain of #9-930?" A direct question.

Her eyes met her superior's as she struggled to keep her voice even and calm. "Yes," was all she replied because that was all that was needed.

"You realize that this boy was selected after very careful deliberation and is one of our unusual special cases?" Another direct question. #43 repeated her answer.

"And here I thought that you were ready for promotion. No, you mislabeled this one." The Trainer's eyes stared straight at her CEO, who saw a tear develop and threaten to roll down the girl's cheek. No time for that, the CEO thought and moved on.

"You were trained to recognize when boys would have to make significant sacrifices for the benefit of the Company. You were *taught* to spot when a particular boy might be on that path. You were *shown* how to *identify* incorrigible hires. And you did not *comprehend* when one was kneeling in front of you." Her eyes bore into #43's as the tear finally escaped from her eye and rolled down her cheek.

The CEO grew increasingly impatient. It was time to finish Naming and get the boys ready to arrive at HQ for Intake.

"His name shall be #9-908," the CEO concluded as the Head Trainers drew a big breath at the sentence she pronounced on the boy formerly known as Evan. To be given an "8" at naming meant that a boy would lose his cock as well as balls, so unimportant that they were rarely mentioned, to benefit the Company and live in the Eunuch dorm to be used as she saw fit. The women left the CEO's private car and imagined what was in store for the arrogant new hire.

She owned all of them: the new hires, the trainers, the Company, the facilities, every rule, training methods and down to their souls. And unless Evan's training was successful, his cock and balls would just fill another jar in the eunuch room closet, located just off the

Medical wing and would sit next to all the other jars of genitals the CEO took from boys who could not be trained to her satisfaction.

Chapter 20

Henry's Night

First Afternoon became First Night and it was the traditional conclusion of the First Training day that all new hires endured on day one of the two-day train trek to HQ. The daytime trainers were inspected by #34's staff before they were permitted to begin training the boys. Their afternoon training session was individualized for each new hire and aimed at eliminating their undesirable baggage. Each Trainer would reveal her training strategies after the new hires were deposited at HQ. First Training afternoon was a big factor when the CEO evaluated which of her staff deserved a promotion.

First Night's lesson would teach the boys how their days and nights would unfold for the rest of their lives. The "rest of their lives" would be drilled into their brains time and time again during the two-day trek. Each boy reacted differently but for the most part, they struggled when the meaning of "forever" began to seep into their brains. That's why First Night was critical to the CEO's training strategy. She enjoyed watching their faces contort into horror when they absorbed what the rest of their lives meant.

Henry was the most pathetic, #71 thought when she stepped into his chilly cell. More pitiful than most of her prior broken boys. His ass was on the floor and his arms were grasping his knees and the boy was sniffling. Apparently, he was trying to gather a last vestige of false bravado and tried to ignore her entry.

That lasted about 10 seconds.

Using a single word command, she ordered him to stand and he performed with a mere two-second delay. First, Henry pulled himself to his hands and knees and then struggled into an erect position. *A good start,* she thought. But it was not fast enough.

"Ship-shape," she demanded almost unnecessarily but mostly to make him react to her single word that she drew from navy experience. He stiffened his shoulders. It was enough for #71 for the first 20 seconds of First Night. But now it was time to make him see what the rest of his life would be like and what discipline and especially obedience meant for him.

She snapped goggles over his eyes, tightened the strap, pressed ear buds into his ears and pushed a button that started the video. He was the only one who could see and hear the clip that was customized by Psych just for him.

#71 stepped back to watch the boy's body react to what he was seeing and hearing. She remembered her own video and a slight tremble ran through her.

The video team always included the required Company-wide critical scenes but edited each video particularly for each new hire. Henry, who was used to ordering around a team of web developers and criticized their code even when it worked perfectly, watched the web workers at the Company add a new feature to the internal site that was to be used by the HR Intake team. This new addition to the intranet enabled the team to evaluate the current trek to the train with better and faster tools and a friendlier UI. There were simple forms that fed into an algorithm that rated the entire Intake process, from delivery to the moment the train started moving, the step that defined the beginning of the trek. Experienced programmers built a multipart online form with back-end integration; the job of the corral of developers he was watching was to install it into the back-end and make sure it was intuitive to use.

Ordinarily, Henry would never perform that task; it was below his dignity. He would hire and supervise a woman to do it. But what he saw in the video was his face superimposed on a naked male worker in the coding pen and a woman leaning over his shoulder inspecting his code as he was writing it. He heard her issue orders for changes and realized she was instructing him to edit his code. Surrounding him were more males being led on leashes away from the coding pen. He was suddenly alone in the web coding area, his naked ass spread across a bright red rubber ball that was his only seat. A corpulent woman whose breasts practically spilled onto his shoulder continued to tell him what he had to do to fix the display. He wanted to gag.

"You'll be fed when you've finished and it's perfect," he heard her hiss into his ear. Her breasts were now bouncing on his skin. He wanted to bite one to teach her a lesson.

Instead, alone in the coding pen, Henry saw on the video that his forehead broke out in a sweat. He could barely breathe being that close to her enormous breasts. And giving him orders! And holding his food hostage! He could barely contain his body's shivering in anger.

Back in the cell, #71's long hair swayed as she watched him tremble. Her brown skin glowed with pleasure as she forced a tube up his unsuspecting ass. With a practiced twist, she pressed him onto a red ball with his asscheeks spread exactly like what he saw on the video. The ball drove the plug deeper into his ass.

From behind his goggles, Henry shuddered against the sudden cold that enveloped his cell as he watched himself do the same thing on the video. The bitch had lowered the heat and he was alone, forced to make changes to his own code while balancing on a stupid red ball while, all by himself. He watched his doppelganger shiver alone in the web workers' pen.

Boys owned by the Company were not allowed to show anger. They had to learn total submission fast to survive and practice it constantly. There were no stress-reduction sessions, no gathering of boys with beer and football and certainly no sassy back talk to their superiors. This is the lifetime of submission that the video taught Henry.

When he thought his balls were going to freeze into icicles, the scene in the video suddenly shifted.

His face was again superimposed on a boy's body and Henry saw himself in a dark room with dozens of other naked men. When his eyes focused, he saw a long white-tiled floor and walls with the same boring texture. Henry was smack in the middle of a sea of male nakedness. Water abruptly started spewing from every side of the room, including downspouts from the top and upward spouts in the floor. He watched the other boys flop on the floor and twist and roll to cover themselves with as much water as possible as fast as they could. The Henry in the cell could not comprehend why his own character in the video joined in.

When the cascade of water morphed into white foam, a small sense of understanding leached into his brain. In the reality of his cell on the train, he felt his skin get wet as he continued to view masses of naked men slither and slide on it, rub it into their armpits, groins and between their asscheeks. Henry stood in his cold train cell and suddenly felt slippery soap slather between his toes. Finally, a torrent of what had to be ice water was shot at the foamy mass of men on the video and they spread themselves wide to rinse their asses, under their arms, in their groins all the while twisting to rinse the suds off every part of their bodies.

Finally, mercifully, the scene shifted.

It became nighttime in the video that Henry watched as he saw dozens of naked men of all shapes and sizes lined up at the foot of rows of cots on both sides of a long windowless room. The nude men stood at the foot of their beds, facing each other only inches apart, apparently being put to bed for the night. At the sound of a single command to turn, all the men spun 180-degrees, so their asses almost touched each other.

In his train compartment, Henry sensed his hips swivel as he felt himself parrot what he watched on the video. #71 allowed herself to smile for a moment and made another note on her tablet.

There was an electronic whir in the background and the men, almost as one, spread their legs, bent over and grasped the handles bolted to the sides of their cots. Trainers walked down the line of asses and inserted a thick tube into each one and moved on to impale the next spread ass in line. When they were all inserted, a Trainer signaled and the men's bodies began to shake.

It took Henry a moment to figure it out, but when he finally did, his brain almost exploded in shock. Their asses were being filled with something – something very evil – that made them shake with pain. They remained there for too long, Henry worried, and after what seemed like forever, the Trainer signaled and another electronic sound filled his ears.

The floor! He saw the floor behind them fall away and the men grabbed the handles tighter and lowered their asses toward the dark pit.

The speed of Henry's breathing, which #71 was measuring, suddenly increased. *He's gotten to the good part*, she surmised.

When the pack of men let their bowels loose and gang-shit into the pit, #71 released the aromatic that duplicated the smell on the video and Henry gagged over and over until he fell to his knees and dry-heaved toward the cell floor. She allowed that to continue for a good two-to-three minutes before she aired out the cell and removed her clean-air mask.

The video concluded with Henry's face atop a nameless male worker as he crawled into his cot and covered himself with a thin blanket. The lights were shut off and the video became a black room. He heard a single noise and he recognized it straightaway: one man sobbing. He never figured out if that was on the video as well, but he knew it came from his own throat.

#71 waited a few minutes for the last sentence of the video to play out. The dark finale was always an emotional moment for new boys. Henry heard the voiceover say, "Welcome to the rest of your life."

She removed his goggles and earphones and ordered him to look up at her from his knees.

Trainers were allowed to utter a single sentence at the end of First Night and #71 was happy to pronounce it now.

"The rest of your life," she reiterated. Then without even a nod to the naked kneeling #3-729, she turned and walked out of the room. Henry heard the door lock behind her. He would learn his name tomorrow during Morning Day Training.

Cory's Night

The CEO's #54, who was the daily Trainer given the boy named Cory to train during the trek to HQ, was eager to begin First Night with him. After his initial breaking session that made him realize that his balls were hers from now on, along with his First Training where thick testicle and asscheek hair was ripped off with violent waxing, Cory lay limp on the cold cell floor. It did not matter that he was a former trained athlete; Cory was mentally exhausted and in real physical pain. He could not even fake his self-comforting bravado. That was how #54 anticipated he would look and she was not surprised. She rarely was.

First Night always brought boys to their rawest – their bodies had been tortured, their angry reactions to pain ignored, their protestations disregarded and their considerable fear about what might happen next was completely discounted. #54's first job at the Company was to plan conferences and meetings for the Teams at HQ. Those events showed her how to pay attention to the smallest details. During Cory's First Night training, she would train him to become observant about every detail the rest of his life held in store.

As he lay flaccid on the cell floor, she gathered the four cuffs attached to chains from each corner and locked a cuff to each ankle and wrist. Tapping her tablet, the chains retracted and all 6'5" of Cory was splayed toward each corner of the cell. She pulled back the cuffs until he was spread-eagle across his cubicle. His dark mocha skin gleamed against the concrete floor

His spread ass faced her.

#54 locked video goggles across his eyes and pressed the ear pods in firmly. Shaking her long blonde hair behind her shoulders, she stood back to watch.

Cory's video was edited by Psych to exaggerate his fears and the first sounds he heard were buzzing voices. Then an image emerged of a room full of women seated at banquet tables. A bell clanged and suddenly naked males crawled into the room. To his horror, Cory saw trays of food on their backs in what had to be a macabre delivery system. The serving boys crept in a straight line toward each table and the women chose their appetizers from the proffered choices. After each selection, they slapped each server's ass to order them to move on. Only then were the server boys released to crawl to serve the next woman at the table.

His mouth fell open when the scene zoomed in on one big black man crawling clumsily behind the others. When that boy turned his face toward the camera it revealed his own face decorating the body that was creeping, serving, being slapped and continuing down the line. He had become a self-propelled serving tray! His real body shivered in his cell as he watched his video body do the same thing. As he watched his ass on the video raise up to steady his tray, his real ass was pulled up in the cold cell. To his horror, he watched the tray in the video threaten to slide off his back. His arms, stretched across his cell, flexed uselessly against the cuffs and chains as he failed to steady it.

The clatter in his ears and the scene before his eyes terrified him: he had dropped the tray!

In the video, a woman moved toward him and beat his ass with a short-handled whip. His raised ass in the reality of the train cell felt stroke after stroke land on his asscheeks as he heard his own voice on the video screaming in pain. Within his cell, #54 heard him whimper and knew exactly what part of the video he was watching. The serving boy was dragged from the banquet room and forced into a cell where the walls began to close in around him. In his train cell, Henry felt the floor and ceiling press against his chest and ass as they likewise compressed on his almost-flat body. In the video, a woman pulled down a small opening in the wall and smiled at his terrorized and face. Cory saw the boy sobbing and in his cell, his eyes released their own tears.

In the video, Cory saw that his replica's cell walls had multiple openings so any woman could approach, reach in and torture him at her will. He was spread eagle and hog-tied to the cell's corners and could not resist any intrusion at all. Woman after woman came by, slapped his balls, whipped his ass and put steel-tooth clamps on his nipples. The video pain was becoming real as #54 hoisted him vertically and inflicted each punishment he saw on the video directly on him in real time.

Whatever he saw happen in the video; he felt it inflicted onto his body in the cell on the train. There was nothing he could do to escape. No choices. No options. Cory screamed.

#54 smiled. *Oh, he must be on the wall,* she figured. Just to make his experience all the more real, she whipped his real ass and drew bright red welts on his hairy backside. Just to reinforce the lesson, she shocked his testicles once or twice so he would take the lesson more seriously.

When the video scene shifted, Cory saw his video counterpart naked in a room while one after another, the event staffers walked in. Each woman was full-bosomed, sported a large belly and very hairy pussy that was almost hidden by their belly overhangs. He was restrained, like the other men in the room, on his hands and knees and locked to the floor.

Cory hated fat women. He was sickened when he imagined having sex with them. In the video, each large woman walked toward one man or another and a speaker issued a single-word command.

"Suck."

Cory could not believe he was being ordered to suck the pussy of women who looked like that! He had never been with a large woman – he always chose the thin blondes – but was facing the most enormous hairy pussy he had ever seen.

In his cell, Cory recoiled, at least the little bit that his hog-tied restraints allowed. #54 did not miss the small movement and she pressed a carefully designed training tool into his face. The skin-like device was covered in pussy hair strands and just for effect, the staff had sprayed it with stank oil. The Cory in the video and the one hog-tied in the cell were both facing the same challenge: follow the command or be punished. He was realizing that all women, no matter if they were fat and hairy, had absolute control over him. He felt bile rise from his gut and he wanted to vomit.

First Training earlier that day taught Cory that obeying would hurt less than the certain punishment he would endure. He saw that the video showed Cory sucking and gagging, sucking and gagging. He knew that if he did not perform in his real train cell, the video character would be whipped into obedience. Cory began to fear that his real ass would again taste #54's tawse.

During his First Night, #54 inflicted every punishment shown in the video onto Cory's burning ass, sore cock and tortured balls, tender nipples and every other part of his body that was stretched across his cell. First Night was designed to teach new boys that their lives were in the hands of their trainers and #54's blonde hair, white skin and inviting pussy defined a new place in his world view. Instead of being a woman he could bed and toss away, he began to see that she controlled his pain. Cory quickly forgot that he ever felt pleasure with a woman.

She let the video wrap up toward blackness as he watched women torture his look-alike and heard his own screams in his ears. #54 watched his balls jiggle in terror when he heard the video's final comment, "Welcome to the rest of your life."

She unhooked him and let him flop onto his belly on the floor. He did not know which part of his body he wanted to caress first – every inch of his skin was on fire and his ass, cock, balls and nipples were only beginning to realize her torture's impact. #54 removed the goggles and earbuds and as she stepped out of his cell, turned and said, "This is the rest of your life.

When the door locked behind her, she was sure she heard him sob.

Oliver's Night

After her promotion to #67, the former #84 strode into Oliver's cell to begin First Night training. Her own training taught her that First Night is the natural culmination of First Day and she appreciated how full-circle the new boys' initial introduction to their new lives was concluding. She loved her part in perpetuating the cycle and bringing honor to her role at the Company

Oliver, who would be known as #6-437 for the rest of his life, was crumpled in a fetal position on the cell floor. His ass, violated by a tech boy wearing an electronic fake cock that morning, felt like it was ablaze. His balls, savaged by the Trainer's electric gun, were almost too sore for him to touch but the thick oval mittens they wrapped around his hands prevented any meaningful soothing. All he could do was hug himself and then flop on the floor trying to make his ass and cock stop burning.

It was a useless endeavor. As Oliver floundered around the floor, #67 marched into his cell and gave the single word command, "Damare!" Her Japanese order needed no translation. Oliver struggled to his feet even though he was not sure what she just said. She smiled slightly that on this First Day, Oliver would respond to her command in whatever language she used. He did not need to understand it; rather, he simply needed to obey.

He was desperate to stroke his balls. On this First Night, he would learn the painful truth that he would never be allowed to touch them again.

Wrapping the goggles around his head and jamming the earbuds in place, #67 pressed the button that started Oliver's carefully edited video. He jumped when the stereo sound blasted into his ears.

"Boys are fucked daily at the Company during training," a strong female voice stated directly into his earbuds.

The prescribed Company training for new hires who were renamed with a leading "4" was to overcome their malingering tendencies by converting how they detested having their asses fucked into a soul-fulfilling submission with every part of their bodies to their new owner. Because Oliver was named with a "4," he was destined to receive daily ass-fucking by anyone and at any time his trainers chose. It would become part of his new life-long experience. And it started right now.

His video opened with a row of boys crouching in front of low tables on which several monitors were arranged. The equipment was first-rate, Oliver noted, and then he saw that none of the boys had chairs. Each was in an uncomfortable crouch with their asses spread but their fingers dutifully typing on keyboards. It dawned on him that was how these men worked. Seatless, uncomfortable and focused.

A woman approached one of the workers in the second row and stood behind him. Oliver watched his fingers slow down from his apparent discomfort of being overseen. Her long black hair hung over her leather vest and almost touched her thong-split ass. Oliver was momentarily distracted by how that thong might make his own burning ass feel a little better.

He saw the boy on the video whose fingers stopped as the narrator's voice said, "His superior locked his keyboard. The Company does not tolerate distraction."

Oliver saw the boy's legs, obviously aching from his forced crouch, begin to spasm. He heard the boy's voice rise to an agonizing pitch. He was screaming loudly and to his surprise, Oliver saw that none of the other workers even glanced at him. The voice continued.

"Company boys work in silence. They do not talk and the Company keeps them quiet with custom noise-cancelling ear plugs that allow no incoming noise except a supervisor's voice. Screaming is pointless." The boy's screeching and squealing fell on literally deaf ears and the voice instructed him again.

"Each boy in the Company tech corral works all day, every day with an implanted ass rod which instructs them when to begin or stop, stand or squat, code or cease immediately to listen for additional instructions. None needs to chat with any other boy; their instructions are delivered via their ass plugs."

Oliver's real-life mouth fell open and his Trainer expertly inserted a spreader gag to reinforce that boys at the Company never talk or are listened to. Shouting and shrieking are ignored. So are questions.

His shoulders suddenly felt heavy. #67 engaged the rods that pressed him into a real-life squat that mimicked the video he was watching. As he was pushed toward the floor, he felt a pointed rod touch his red-hot ass and insert itself with his own body weight as he was forced lower and lower into an agonizing crouch. The boy he saw on the screen was shrieking in an incredible decibel level of pain and Oliver gulped when he realized what would happen to the boy – and to himself – next.

The rod pressed deeper into his ass than he believed possible. It moved up and down, up and down, in a regular motion that he echoed with his own movement caused by #67 pressing a key on the wall panel that moved the metal rods above and below his armpits into motion. Horrified that he was self-fucking the rod in his ass, Oliver moaned in pain and fell into a state of wretched humiliation.

She changed the rod's tempo to parallel the video. Still screaming uselessly, the video boy humped his own rod while Oliver fucked the one shoved into his ass. His quadriceps aching, Oliver bleated in pain equal to the indignation that coursed through him. #67 timed the scene and when the video changed focus, she abruptly stopped the rod's motion. Oliver remained in a forced crouch with his ass painfully close to the cold cell floor. And the rod was still stuck way up his ass.

The video continued and the voice began. "Company technology is advanced and hyper secure. Workers receive daily training to learn new skills and keep our systems in the finest working order and protected from intrusion." For a moment, Oliver was relieved and almost looked forward to working with bleeding edge technology. That feeling lasted until the video voice started up again.

"Boys are not allowed to work with advanced schema and equipment until they are proven well-trained. They are schooled and re-educated until they pass Company required performance tests." The scene shifted and Oliver watched a room full of boys kneeling on circular risers in an otherwise empty room. The boys' ankles and wrists were locked to the floor and each boy's face was pressed into the ass crack of the boy in front of him. On the higher riser, a circle of boys was similarly locked only this group had been placed into alternating positions. One boy was flat on his back, the next on his hands and knees straddling the lower boy with his face pressed into his cock. The highest tier was a circle that combined both: a boy locked on his back, a boy with his face pressed into his cock and a third boy behind him with his arms locked around the kneeler's waist. Each pair or trio of boys was one in a set that dotted each tier in the room.

Every boy was fully engaged, whether on his back, his tongue in an asshole or his genitals locked into a kneeler. It was then Oliver saw the flesh-colored strap circling their hips. Every boy was tied into a skin-tight harness with a huge molded cock protruding from it. The voice in his ears was relentless.

"No boy at the Company is allowed either erection or orgasm," she said clearly. Company training is perfect at educating boys how they behave for the rest of their lives." Before he could digest the ominous warning, the boys on the video began moving.

Each boy on his back opened his lips and drove his tongue into the ass pressed into his face. Each kneeler sucked the fake cock worn by the supine boy and each boy behind the kneelers pressed their fake cocks into the asshole in front of them. They all moved slowly as the voice described the training.

"Each boy has a chip inserted in a permanent ring that he wears behind his balls. The chip was developed by the Company Medical team to communicate silently with the tech staff. Boys are moving in perfect rhythm with the chip's instructions. As we change the speed…" the voice trailed off but Oliver watched the incredible scene in the video. The rhythm increased in speed. Every boy soundlessly fucked or sucked faster. The voice added, "We control the boys' speed. Workers simply perform as their ass rods instruct them."

The circles of fucking and sucking males worked faster and faster with each boy performing perfectly in the macabre tempo that was regulated by a chip inserted in a ring that pierced each boy's frenum. Oliver gagged when he imagined how long and how much testing went into the chip's design because he finally understood that one would be inserted behind his own cock and balls.

Just before the video ended, #67 pressed a device between Oliver's asscheeks that sent a bolt of pain throughout his entire body. It was a well-tested alternative to a local anesthetic, and it took several minutes for Oliver to realize a ring had been inserted into his tender frenum by a robotic apparatus. He screamed at the pain and the intrusion but like all boys' noises at the Company, no one heard his protestations. His Trainer knew that the real ring would be inserted when the train reached the Company HQ and they were handed off to Medical and Intake. This one was only temporary.

The video voice continued unsparing. "Welcome to the rest of your life."

She disengaged all the support rods and Oliver crashed to the floor in a heap of delirium. As she turned to leave his cell, #67 remarked, "The rest of your life."

Although they monitored all the new boys on the train all night, no one kept a record of how long he sobbed before falling into a fitful sleep.

James's Night

He was used to sleeping on a cold floor, just like he knew what it was like to be watched all the time, intruded upon without warning, inspected naked in front of others and roused from a deep sleep to be used for someone's purpose. To cope with the banality of prison, James learned to be as inconspicuous as possible as he could while he lived in a herd of thousands of convicted men. At first, he hated prison. Over time, it became normal; he never let himself rebel.

A solidly built black man, James did everything he could to lower his profile in prison just so he could survive. He learned to cope with prison rape – the crime he had been convicted of and the sentence he was serving – and after a while, could pretty much guess when it was going to happen. He taught himself how to breathe through it and allow his sphincter to relax just enough to endure it without damage. The CEO's teams had studied James's story before recommending him as a new hire. She watched his videos multiple times to see for herself how he managed the insanity that he lived in. She assigned #62 to train James because she physically resembled the full-bodied woman James believed he had the right to beat and rape.

The Company often needed experienced tradespeople to keep the boys' showers, tubs, toilets and shit pits in top working order. If he worked out, James might eventually get promoted and be allowed to work on the female staff's spa area and all the complicated plumbing needs in the Estheticians' wing. Only a few boys at HQ were allowed to work on – or even know about – the CEO's private bath. She was not sure James would ever rise to that level of trust because, she surmised, he did not care if he did. All James wanted was to do his job and go home where some food might be in the refrigerator next to a cold six-pack or a box of wine.

His attitude needed overhauling on many levels. That was the core of her plan for him.

When #62 glanced at the small monitor outside his compartment, she saw what she expected: a spent black body curled on the floor breathing in a measured rhythm. She anticipated that James was calming himself from the torture of First Training. Psych had taught her that initial looks were deceiving so she studied him a few seconds longer, starting with his toes.

They twitched and she caught it. Then it was his fingers and she noted that slight movement, too. Checking one body part after another that showed the slightest movement was exactly what #62 was looking for. He was desperate to find any bit of calmness, but his body would not allow it. The twitches were his tell. Armed with that knowledge, she walked in.

With her big stomach hanging over her Company-issued thong and her breasts glomming out of the leather vest with its dials and buttons, one of James's eyes saw her and could not help but stare at her blonde hair. He knew better than to look at a white woman anywhere except in her eyes.

When she bent over him, her breasts flopped completely out of the vest and hung next to his sweaty skin. She leaned closer to his face and dangled them intentionally no more than an inch from his eyes.

"Time," she said in a Single Word Command and waited for him to interpret that it was an order to stand. She counted time while James struggled to gain his footing.

Too long, she thought, and noted it on her tablet.

Visions of the morning sessions spiraled through James's thoughts as he rose and stood as straight as possible. He watched her stalk around him, survey every one of his body parts, lift one of his arms and drop it, stretch his asscheeks and let them flop closed, swat his cock and slap his aching balls. She inspected him like a prize heifer at auction. Finally, she forced his jaws apart and pushed an expander between his teeth. He heard it crank as his jaw was forced open. His gut contracted.

With the boy now silenced, she wrapped goggles around his eyes and snapped them shut. Now blind, James felt her cover his ears with silence when the she inserted the earbuds. He heard loud music at first and then a distant voice.

"You are assigned to Facilities," the voice said. "You will be trained to provide maintenance services for the staff and work to become the best plumber to benefit the Company."

James shifted his feet while #62 watched the tremors that coursed through him.

The video showed a white-tiled shower room with dozens of high and low shower heads. The walls were dotted with more spigots that could shoot water from every angle. Hoses with spray handles were locked onto clamps on every wall. James imagined that at least 100 people could use this shower room at the same time. A siren clanged and men rushed in from every door and stood in the center of the shower room. Another siren sounded and water rushed in from every angle as the men stood ramrod still until everyone of them was drenched.

He saw their penises and balls shrink into almost nothing and was horrified to learn that the water had to be ice cold.

Another siren clanged and women in Lycra bras and thong-like panties moved in. They wielded long-handled brushes and soaped the men everywhere. They talked casually with each other, ignoring the person or the body part they were brushing. They scrubbed a face or legs or scrotum with the same force and then moved to the next boy.

"You will maintain the showers," the voice said. "And you will clean the pits."

The video shifted to another white-tiled room where two rows of boys were lined up with their hands locked into O-rings that were secured on the wall. There were cuffs secured just above their knees.

"Boys are cleaned inside and out. Your job will be to maintain the equipment and ensure the pits are empty."

James heard an electronic motor whir and pull their legs up and behind them so they were hanging upside down from the ceiling while their arms were still shackled to the wall. Women walked around the platform and inserted thick tubes into every rectum, one after another, as they chatted casually with one another. The hoses were opened and James knew that those men's assholes were being filled with something that made them all scream at the same time. No one had to tell him how much the evil liquid must have hurt. The leg lifts shook them up and down and another round of liquid was forced into their asses. Their pained cries filled his ears and brain as the women retraced their steps, removing the tubes and inserting a fat black rubber plug into each rectum one at a time, as they walked down the line.

"The pits are the primary part of your function at the Company," the voice said.

After too many minutes of begging and pleading by the dangling men with overfilled rectums, James watched them all get lowered and then twisted so they remained suspended a few feet above the floor. Their rectum plugs had short cords, just within reach of the chatting women. He gritted his teeth and screamed, "NO!" silently because his jaw spreader prevented anything but grunts from leaving his throat.

The floor fell away. Each woman grabbed two plugs at a time, one from each side of the dangling line, and yanked them out. Then each of them moved on to the next plugged boys.

Dozens of them screamed and out of nowhere, a woman's voice said, "Now."

Cries of joy filled his ears and a horrid vision of almost a hundred asses releasing the evil enemas and whatever else was in their rectums filled his eyes. #62 sprayed the aromatic and he gagged while in the reality of his cell while men group-shit on cue into the fetid shit pit.

"Maintaining the pits will be your focus until you earn a promotion," the voice said. James's heart pounded, his breathing sped up and none of his relaxation techniques were working. His whole body shook in horror.

"You will also keep the urinals in perfect order," the voice went on relentlessly.

A new scene unfolded inside his goggles and James saw men running into a different white-tiled circular room that had long glass walls dotted with holes. The men stood each in front of their assigned hole and pressed their cocks through them. Their faces were pressed into the grips that held them tightly. They were lined up around the round central glass wall and they only thing they could see were the faces and bodies of the men facing them. They stood in strict silence; their faces pointed at each other's cocks. Then a bell rang.

It was their cue! The whole group struggled to start peeing at the same time and it was obvious that some were having difficulty getting their piss to start. James had seen that before in prison when they obviously drugged their food with pee inhibitors so the prisoners wouldn't ask for bathroom breaks too often. In the video, just to make it worse, the women stood behind them, taunted the boys who could not make their pee start and threatened them with ending the pee break early so their cocks would have to be plugged with training caps attached to metal sounds until the next time scheduled for peeing. Some of the women tased their balls that were pressed into the glass wall with miniature shock rods so some men were screaming in pain and trying to pee at the same time.

Despite his jaw spreader, James grunted and felt an insane urge to pee. Right there, right on the floor of his cell, with that big-breasted blonde watching. He fought to control his bladder and watched the video where men became hysterical trying to pee on cue while their balls were being shocked.

She knew where he probably was in the video and #62 dipped his hand into a bowl of warm water.

He could not stop it; he peed straight down his legs and felt the warm liquid seep between his toes. When the men on the video could not stand it anymore, they started to fall, but their penises were locked into the tubes and they flailed uselessly at the glass walls for support.

"Maybe we should just cut them off," he heard a woman's say as the others laughed.

"Welcome to the rest of your life," the narrator said as his goggles went black.

Within moments, the eye and ear coverings were removed, and James crumpled to the cold hard cell floor. He managed to open one eye and heard #62 say over her shoulder toward him while exiting, "The rest of your life."

Despite his aching jaws from which she had just yanked out the spreader, James screamed.

Evan's Night

He was furious, sore, humiliated, hungry and cold. His nipples were screaming in pain and he was forced to waddle with his legs spread when he tried to walk. Although he had felt the three rings attached between his legs, Evan's mind was reeling. In the cold dank cell on this interminable train ride from hell, he could barely remember applying to that want ad that grabbed his attention that Sunday morning that seemed several lifetimes ago.

He did not know yet that the rings were temporary until the CEO decided whether to keep him. If she dropped him at a small railroad station, naked and without identification, the chip inside those rings allowed law enforcement to track him. She made sure that several people would report him missing and the authorities would be sent their GPS tracker anonymously.

He tried crouching to relieve the pain from the piercings but no position was remotely comfortable. He investigated the three metal rings and realized they were welded shut. Even though he had no hope of success, Evan tried kneeling with his legs spread and that predictably provided no relief. He could not lay down on the cold floor without searing pain emanating from his ass. He could not get comfortable at all. That made him angrier.

When #36 finished observing him through the screen outside his cell and saw him unable to find even basic human comfort, she punched in her code and strode into the room. Without any hesitation, she ordered him to his feet.

Evan grumbled, "Hey! This hurts! I want a doctor and I want him now!"

Her thick lips stayed straight as she assessed his demand. The boy not only demanded a doctor but used the word "him" to define a medical staffer. #36 realized she had a lot of work to do to turn him into a proper worker or he was destined to suffer the fate of the few hires who had also been named with the ominous "8" that often led to cock and ball amputation. Eunuchs were not actively sought out by the Company but they behaved and followed orders well so the CEO kept a few of them around.

He was no match for her physically. #36 was tall, big-boned and her ebony skin reflected brilliantly from the strong overhead light. In spite of his regular trips to the gym, Evan was what the CEO called a "fancy boy," a young-ish self-proclaimed "mogul" who spent too much time staring into his phone and not enough time learning how to respect women and perform what they demanded from him.

She hauled him to his feet and pressed his legs together. He groaned behind gritted teeth. #36 tugged on his newly pierced nipple rings and ignored his screams of pain. Her strong hand dug between his thighs and grabbed one of his frenum rings. Tugging it in an agonizing rhythm, she watched Evan's eyes fill with tears and his throat swallow with guttural gasps.

When she let go, he tried to fall to the floor, but she pulled the nipple rings and stood him up again quickly while he let loose with an ear-splitting shriek. It stopped only after she locked the goggles around his eyes and pressed the earbuds in place.

A cacophony of sound filled Evan's ears. No narrator, no voice, no guide explained what he was seeing. He stopped sobbing to let his eyes dry so he could focus on the video. The first scene finally came into focus and Evan tried uselessly to scream louder.

There had to be at least 100 naked men laying on the floor of a white-tiled room. Some were on their backs; others flat on their stomachs. But all of them had rods protruding from their asses that had to be at least three feet long. He stared at the rods and then back at the mass of black, brown and white skin that made up the horrific diversity of the group. Women entered the room and jiggled several of the rods as if to test their depth and tightness. It was then that the lights in the white-tiled room dimmed.

Evan had to focus harder to see what was going on in the low-lit scene. He heard no voices; rather, he felt that some movement was taking place and he heard the distinctive sounds of flesh flopping on the floor. When he could focus a little more, he saw that the women were spraying the men with hoses but what the men did was stunning. They flattened themselves, rolled over and over and pressed their faces into the goo. They seemed to want the substance to cover every part of their bodies. The stomach-layers rotated themselves as did those flat on their backs, but they always stayed in their assigned positions with those damned rods protruding three feet out of their asses. Evan did not know what they did, but he despised those rods.

Another gush of oily gel shot from the women's hoses and the men performed their macabre choreography again – rolling and thrashing in the now four-inch deep river of ooze that was filling the room. This time they put their heads into it to make sure their bald heads were fully covered with the awful stuff. There was not an inch of their skin that was not covered in whatever the women were discharging throughout the room.

And then, in an instant, it was over.

The woman secured their hoses and started stacking the oily men on top of each other, ass-to-face. Using the rods as handles, they led a stomach-layer on top of a back-layer, alternating them black, brown and white. Forcing each man to the ever-growing top of the pile, the gooey men had to climb however they could manage to reach the top of the human pile. It did not matter where they stepped – on a chest, hips, face or cock. Eventually the women got stacks of six men arranged all around the room and ran straps around the piles and tied them into neat packages. The lights came back on and the goo drained from the floor.

The woman who appeared to be in charge said, "Time." Just that. One word.

Despite his pain, Evan's mind exploded as he was petrified of what might happen to the stacks of naked human flesh. His body spasmed in fear as his own pain was almost forgotten. *Time?* he wondered. Time for what? After a few more seconds of video, it became clear.

As if on cue, women stood at both ends of each pile and grasped one rod after another and twisted them. The piles of men shrieked in unison. Their horrible pain was obvious and they began thrashing their asses in useless attempts to escape the torture.

The room full of piles of naked bound men began undulating as one.

They heaved and surged while Evan absorbed their screaming and screeching. He drank in their pain as the entire room devolved into a mass of motion punctuated only by animalistic growls. He heard the flopping of oily skin against a lower body. One ass rocked hard up and down, back and forth as if beckoning toward him. That's when Evan realized his video had morphed in 3D. Asses were humping inches from his face. Open-mouthed screams fed into his ears and their contorted faces exploded in and out of his field of vision. Whatever those rods shot into those 100 asses was something Evan learned must be feared. His body cringed reflexively each time a screaming mouth or humping ass was driven toward his eyes. He shared their pain with his own agonized nipples and from the set of rings welded between his legs. He knew their bawling and squawking because he had been reduced to that earlier in the day. At least he thought it was the same day. Evan was growing deathly afraid of what tomorrow might bring. If he survived the night.

After what seemed like hours, the mountains of bodies' movement slowed and the screaming lessened. Piles of men were scooped onto forklifts and they were driven toward a metal double door. A woman typed in a code and the door swung open to reveal another pristine white room arranged with medical exam tables. The first forklift of men dropped its load while women untied the straps. Each male was propelled to a table by a woman driving his rectal rod. When the six tables were full and their inhabitants locked into place by their ankles, wrists and forehead bands, a woman approached each table.

Evan saw in the distance that the other packages of male flesh were delivered, stacked in piles, awaiting their turns.

Each woman grasped an electric razor and shaved each man's head. Formerly groomed hair fell in gobs to the floor and Evan thought he heard several of them sob.

Silently, they raised the men's legs up and spread them far apart. Their asses were lifted off the tables making their rods even easier to reach. What Evan did not realize yet was that this wing of the Company's HQ was known as Esthetics. And it was the Estheticians that performed the near final step before new hires were assigned to their internships for first evaluations.

The CEO permitted no identifiable physical traits on her workers. Not even hair. Besides, she knew that it helped reduce any latent competition among male staff.

Let them see themselves as I see them. Bald.
Hairless. Unfettered by clothing, status or class.
Simple flesh to be used.

Evan was spellbound by how quickly the women worked. They slathered on hot wax, pressed gauze into it and ripped off all the hair on the men's legs. Several screamed out loud while others gritted their teeth and tried to endure the hot pain.

Then they did the same thing on their chests, stomachs and finally reached their genitals. Longer hair was cut with scissors and tossed to the floor. Then the women brought magnifying lights to inspect the new boys' crotches.

First they applied hot wax, let it set and then stripped off pubic hair in long continuous strokes. By now, the room was a cacophony of screeching, crying men whose pain was ignored by every woman in the Esthetics theater. Because the CEO demanded completely denuded males, the estheticians peered into their magnifiers and used pointed tweezers to remove every last strand. They tweezed rapidly as the crescendo of agony rose higher.

Evan's ears hurt from the noise. And his own pubis twitched in fear.

The women were relentless. They waxed the workers' underarm hair, shoulders and toes. Using the omnipresent anal rods as handles, they flipped the males onto their knees and waxed every inch of their backs. Evan was certain several of them drew blood.

Finally, they were allowed to stand. The women spread their asses and hooked the protruding rods each into an O-ring that descended from the ceiling. Suddenly, the six men in Evan's field of vision screamed in unison. Whatever was shot into their rectums by those despicable rods, Evan figured, was worse than hell.

The men were hosed clean and Evan finally figured out what the evil goo was in the previous room – pre-waxing skin tightener. A chemical that was designed to make their waxing more painful by tightening their pores. He tried to breathe, to control both his fear and his body's incessant trembling. After the boys were shooed off their tables and hosed clean, a chest bar was locked around each one and they were led to the long wall where they were hooked to tethers. From Evan's vantage, it looked like there were at least a hundred spaces.

The scene shifted. The next pile of six men was untied and locked to the tables where the same evil process was performed. The video caught a few moments of conversation between an Asian woman and a big-boned African American woman, the latter of whom was very tall and sported a very muscular physique. She had big breasts with huge nipples.

"Who's assigned to drop them into their slave quarters?" the Asian woman asked.

"That's my privilege," the other answered. "I'm eager to get their rods locked in place so there won't be any resistance to their new bedding situation." Her thick lips drew into a smile that filled her face. "This is their first experience with group sleep."

Evan's knees buckled when he heard her say "group sleep." His thoughts were jumbled and his rectum constricted when he translated what "group sleep" must mean. And he believed he understood what the ass rods were for. It was confirmed by the voice in his ears.

"Welcome to the rest of your life," was all it said before the video went black. Overwhelmed by the video's predictions, he fell into a fetal position directly at #36's feet.

#36 ripped off the Velcro strap on his goggles and yanked the earbuds out. Evan yelped in fear as she ignored his agony and strode toward the compartment's door. Turning her head slightly toward him, she said, "The rest of your life."

She walked out as Evan curled up on the cold floor and cried like a baby.

Chapter 21

All Company male staffers were fed at the same time throughout the Company's global network of locations. On the train, new hires were fed individually so they could learn their new feeding routine and could easily be punished for missteps without distracting the other new boys. During the train trek to HQ, new boys ate by themselves, supervised by their Trainers. The CEO believed isolation enabled them to get accustomed to how they would be fed for the rest of their lives more efficiently.

The Psych and Intake teams set up feeding schedules for each new hire using criteria from the Medical group. They made sure there was enough nutrition, special needs were addressed, and dietary plans put in place. They determined that James would go on the 'fat boy' plan and would be fed a lower-calorie, high protein diet to force weight loss without his suffering from diminished strength. They ordered the same 'skinny boy' diets for Henry and Oliver – full of protein, a heavy dose of vegetables with a hunk of fiber. Medical determined that both of the skinny tech boys apparently ate poorly – mostly junk food and sodas while they were working. As expected, Cory's prior diet was rich in cholesterol and lowering that was the focus of his Company 'rich boy' diet.

That left Evan who was obviously used to fine dining, organic foods and healthy snacks. Medical set up his 'frat boy' diet to include skinless chicken, fish and no beef but featuring roughage because although Evan was loathe to admit it, he was often constipated. Medical had observed him straining in the bathroom on covert video that the CEO had made prior to hiring him. Every boy's bathrooming was available for the CEO or her teams to observe and allowed

Medical to ensure that peeing and shitting were performed on the Company's schedule.

Promptly at 5:45 each evening, all boys were fed. Throughout the Company, boys assembled in the dining hall, took their assigned seats, and were allowed to begin when the monitor gave them a single word command: "Eat." Dinnertime was silent; boys were not allowed to visit or chat with each other while performing tasks. They ate quickly and purposefully because they knew in a very short time, they'd hear the monitor say, "Stop."

At that moment, each boy put his spork down to the left of his plastic tray, stood behind his chair and faced the center of the room while waiting to be led single file to their third bathroom break of the day. They knew there would be only one more that evening and they were eager to pee, even if it meant that the entire male staff was forced to urinate together. The boys who were on constipation diets were more eager to move their bowels in the special area reserved for what the staff had come to call the "dinner poopers."

Medical paid careful attention to the poopers and their product. If a boy's stool was too hard or soft, they adjusted the medication laced in their food and occasionally added a few natural foods, like prunes, to their diets. The Company's staff was provided excellent preventive medical care, down to the food they were permitted to eat and the quality and quantity of what their bowels expelled.

Food was served on numbered plastic trays and food staffers checked each boy's brand before placing a tray in front of them. Company boys' number designations that were assigned during their intake on the train became their identity in all aspects of their work life. To be sure, Hospitality trainers lifted each boy's cock and ball sac to reveal their branded designations so food staff was sure to serve the correct diet to each boy. The boys who were desperate to pee learned to bite their tongues – literally - to prevent leaking when Hospitality lifted their organs to check their brands.

Name branding was always a highly anticipated event at the Company. When new boys were hired, they were renamed for

Company use but female trainer candidates had to earn their numbers from the CEO. Their branding ceremony was a joyful day that was broadcast to all Company locations.

In the training car, the boys brought along for use during the new hire train trek were hanging from a wall until they were needed. For feeding, they were unhooked and led in a silent line to the dining car where they were told to sit at their places at the low table on a platform. They dropped their legs into the recess under it. Reminiscent of Japanese dining, each serving boy placed his naked ass on a clearly marked circle and spread his asscheeks as they would always do at HQ when they were allowed to sit. Their wrists were cuffed and locked to the table sides with short chains that allowed them minimal movement but enough to spoon feed themselves.

When all the plates were delivered, #81, the Hospitality head Trainer, announced, "Eat." Boys struggled against their chains and cuffs and a few managed to insert a spork into their mouths, but most of them were inept and trails of dinner ran down their chins. On the train, #81 was sure to consult with Medical to make sure their diets included soup, stews with sauce and other recipes that challenged their restraints. That made excellent training and it was Hospitality's way of reminding them that they would never excel at even the simplest tasks.

When time was almost up, #81 clicked the Ass Trainer video in the Trainers' car so they could assess each boy's pre-bathroom exercise. A fundamental purpose of eating was to promote bathroom experiences with the outcomes that Medical and Hospitality assigned. Over time, food became unimportant to male staff; it was just something to slog through to get to bathrooming. They were that desperate to pee and shit.

As they tried to manage their sporks of food toward their lips, the silver circles under their asses whirred to life. Rods emerged and their tips sprayed Company-developed lubricant into their rectums. Their indoctrination into the Company meant they occasionally suffered from out-of-sync schedules for either training or when an important work project had to be completed on time. To overcome those schedule anomalies, the CEO and Medical worked with the Ass

Trainers to ensure that the boys used on the train trek were cleaned out regularly after dinner. Constipated boys were cranky and were of less use to the CEO.

Medical assigned #82 to their after-food shitting. She watched their reactions to the lubricant as they sat and tried to eat. Her expertise was in gels and their effects and she made sure every male ass was perpetually lubricated so that when the CEO chose to use any boy's rectum for any purpose, there was no ripping or tearing. Boys' asses had to last the rest of their lives so the CEO could choose any workers at any time for any purpose. Ample lubricant was their new way of life.

For this particular post-food bathrooming, #82 chose a reliable lube infused with irritating herbs that helped stimulate their bowels. Before the train trek, she performed several trials using boys who had just eaten and used those who were between feedings as a control group. Her lab, where she observed boys shitting on one of her many lab-quality toilets, was always a challenge for maintenance workers.

First, she experimented with an essential oil that forced waves of muscle contractions with three boys who had been fed high fiber meals all day. She hung them from their wrists and dropped the floor, so they dangled with their toes just out of reach of the platform. Each had an ass rod inserted, the favorite method of delivery of test gels in her lab at the Company. #82 touched a button and heard the lube flow.

Their faces told her everything she needed to know.

Grimacing in agony, the boys tried to press their legs together to prevent shitting all over their legs and feet. Pressing another button, she dropped the floor out of the way entirely and watched them try to cross their legs and will their asscheeks and sphincters to tighten. After a few more spurts of gel, she studied their faces to evaluate the degree of their struggles and to see how many of them shit on her command.

Some of the boys were screaming and crying and as usual, she ignored it as typical boy behavior.

Finally, she turned off the gel and had her newly-assigned trainee pull out their ass rods. #82 loved having a trainee who was clueless about what could happen in the ass lab.

The new trainee had been hired two train treks ago and this was her first hands-on session with the Ass Trainers. She was eager to please #82 and jumped up to start her task when ordered. She pulled the rods quickly, one after another, and stood awaiting her next assignment.

She never saw it coming.

As if on cue, three boys shit simultaneously. They did not let their shit drip out; instead, they were so eager to relieve their bowels that they humped the air in rapid contractions to make it expel faster. Shit covered their legs and feet and drooled into the floor pit. It sprayed in every direction, including all over the trainee. She was aghast but knew she had to stand her ground because she learned that "the ones who run away never rise up" in the Company ranks.

Watch them when they're surprised. See how they cope with the unexpected. Test them and then test them again.

The dangling boys spewed shit for several minutes and even the exhaust fans could not keep up with the stench they created. #82 worked safely behind her glass enclosure and tried not to laugh at the scene. She knew that the trainee would be gifted her name later that night and this shit-smeared skin experience would be reflected in her number. She would carry this test's memory with her for the rest of her life for as long as she was allowed to work at the Company.

That group of boys was dismissed and maintenance boys began cleaning the Ass Lab. That's when #82 decided to use this time for the second trial: a new lube that had been developed to induce severe itching and create internal contractions as a side benefit. She was eager to try it in a real situation. She ordered four boys to be taken from the wall and hauled into her lab.

This group looked a little newer to #82. Their frightened eyes darted from corner to corner of the white-tiled room to see if they could figure out what was going to happen to them. For her part, #82 enjoyed testing on the new ones. They were so easy to overwhelm, and their reactions were visceral. It helped her evaluate the effects of the chemicals she was testing.

These boys were positioned with their ankles locked and their legs spread wide. Their wrists were locked to an overhead bar. She tapped a button on the wall and the bars whirred toward the floor in front of them and the boys were quickly on their knees with their legs spread and faces kissing the white tile floor.

She only needed to see their asses. She had no use for their faces. Yet.

Even a few Medical staffers tuned in to observe this test. They always wanted to see how new Company chemicals performed. She invited #94 and her staff of trained ass inserters to observe as well. As usual, all tests were videotaped so the CEO was provided the day's highlights after her dinner.

She watched as the newly shit-stained trainee inserted ass rods into each boy. #82 watched to see if the girl seemed interested in any boy's ass or if she hesitated to impale any rectum with a Company approved rod. What mattered to #82 was that the girl learned to ignore an ass and the boy who wore it. She had no time for trainees who were fascinated with butt holes or who hesitated whenever a boy grunted or screamed. To succeed at the Company, a trainee had to learn early on that these were just staff asses and the boys who wore them were meaningless.

The trainee did not disappoint. She drove each rod into one ass after another, quickly and ended with a slight flourish. Once or twice she jiggled a rod to test its depth and was greeted with a groan that she heard about outwardly ignored. The girl had possibilities, #82 noted.

All the cameras were pointed at the boys' exposed asses and a split screen added their faces to a sidebar on their monitors. #82 tapped a button and the new lube she developed shot in. Each injection was greeted by screams muffled by the boys' floor-kissing faces. So far, so good, #82 noted, pressed a button and waited for the next reaction.

Within seconds, the boys' noises bellowed into full-throated screams as the chemicals did their work. Fighting mightily but uselessly against their locked ankles and wrists, the boys could merely thrash up and down within scant inches to try to mitigate the lube's evil process. They humped their asses up and down repeatedly and hopelessly because with every one of their movements, their rods self-inserted more deeply and delivered more of the new chemicals. They began squealing like pigs and every one of them screeched for the evil chemical to stop. #82 knew that if she stood them up and unplugged the rods, they would fill the pit with liquid shit, a nice by-product of the new compound she was working on.

The Medical staffers nodded at what they witnessed and then turned away to refocus on their work. Ass Trainers had seen what they needed to observe and they, too, resumed their work. #82 focused her attention on the trainee to see her reaction to a new situation where the boys she oversaw were obviously in agonizing pain. To her slight annoyance, the girl looked almost like she cared about the boys' plight. That would never do at the Company.

All trainees answered to their superiors every moment of every day. #82 pressed a rarely-used red button and the girl's nipples were set on fire with hot electrical pulses. She repeated it four times, one for each boy, all the while staring at the girl's tearful eyes. She shook her head from side to side.

When she thought the girl had been corrected enough, she stopped the stinging and ordered the girl to put the boys into a crouch with their asses hanging over the well-used shit pit. #82 was eager to see how they would shit with the new lube – achieving the correct quantity and quality were Company standards in all things. Their hands, still attached to the steel bar, were repositioned so they boys were aligned nicely to shit as well as to be observed from all angles.

#82 ordered the rods removed. The trainee obeyed quickly and then jumped back several feet.

Make sure they learn their lessons the first time.
Two lessons is one too many.

Shit flowed in pulses and was very liquid, #82 noted. After a few group ass contractions, she was pleased to see stream after stream of brown shit expelled from each of them. Because these boys were newer to the Company, they were overwhelmed at being used as test rats and a few of them were crying. Again, #82 studied her trainee and was pleased to see her lock her eyes on their asses and not study the overhead screen out of curiosity to see what their faces looked like.

All in all, #82 deemed it a successful test. She recommended the new lube to be used on the boys on the train trek after First Night's dinner.

Back on the train, the boys stood silently in the dining car. The Hospitality head Trainer signaled for the newly-tested lube to be introduced in to them. She watched their faces as they first shrieked in agony and then watched their full-body trembling as they fought with their bowels not to humiliate themselves in front of others in the feeding car. What they did not realize is that the specially-designed rods were tantamount to plugs and no shit would spill until they were in their proper place in the trainee shitting area.

Head Trainers often assigned lower-level trainees to take boys to the train's last car, dubbed the "shit car." She motioned for her girl, a 40-ish year old recent hire who filled the CEO's need for a new ass Trainer, to focus on these boys' most basic task. She specified her preference for the hire; she wanted a short, full-breasted, very plump, with flesh that jiggled when she walked, and above all, stern. A want ad for that position received a record number of applications and this girl topped the list. Her onboarding train trek saw three stations-stops where the CEO discarded one undesirable applicant after another. The girl was tested and she scored surprisingly high.

The girl wore a typical trainee's vest with her huge breasts hanging out the front and her massive belly obliterating any view of her pussy. Trainees wore only a leather strap that split their pussies and ass and attached to the vest's front and back buckles. She bounced happily into position to lead the line of bowel-ready boys to the shit car and all the trainers smiled at her rolls of flesh that jiggled independently as she moved. She pointed to her back, indicating that the boys should follow her, and walked them agonizingly slowly to the shit car as they tried to tighten their sphincters as they marched. A nice touch, #81 thought.

#81 liked her trainee's style. The boys endured the slow trudge with desperate grunts from those needing to expel their bowels immediately. #81 would watch the shit car video later with the other Head Trainers but for now, they retired to the planning area to make sure Second Training Day was ready to go.

It was time to feed the new boys.

Chapter 22

In spite of a day on the train that had turned their worlds upside down as they were indoctrinated into their new roles as Company staff, the new hires were hungry at the end of First Day. They had not been fed since they were forced to drink an unpleasant concoction prior to boarding the train and even though their minds were as exhausted as their bodies, hunger pangs always set in with new boys at the end of First Day.

At the Company, feeding time for boys followed a strict routine and new hires had to learn how they would be fed during their life of work at the Company. Everything they knew yesterday about eating, from being allowed utensils to sitting to eat a plate of food, had to be relearned. They would discover that being granted even a spork to eat with, just like everything else in their new jobs, had to be earned.

The stringent feeding schedule prevented any disruption of their work.

The Wellness Team knew that it was not productive to feed new hires as a group, especially on First Night. The Hospitality, Medical and Psych teams forged a plan to integrate new boys into the Company way of feeding that was adhered to throughout all the Company branches. They regarded feeding time as a short and necessary segment of the staff's day that needed no special decoration. Feeding was part of the functional schedule at the Company.

Boys also had to learn that food was provided without fanfare. They had to learn to eat what was put in front of them. There was no ordering, no menu perusal, no substitutions nor any choices. They ate what was served, finished and were bathroomed by the training staff. Then it was back to work or to bed.

The Medical and Wellness teams worked from the CEO's stipulation that feeding was not a reward; rather, it was merely a few minutes of the staff's day. It was never a social event; chitchat was not allowed. Feeding was a learning experience that would take several weeks to fully ingrain into the new hires. They started learning how it worked on their initial train trek to HQ. Feeding competence was an important section of the CEO's training goals.

The Wellness Team coordinated with the other teams: Hospitality, Medical and Psych. Training new boys as to how they would be fed was a strategy that needed a coordinated four-team effort and was well-tested before receiving approval from the CEO. On this First Night, the feeding Trainers checked their lists and were ready to start. This First Night, boys were fed individually in isolation and never saw or heard the other new hires while learning how to eat. Sometimes the noises new boys made were distracting to other new boys, so soundproof feeding cells became the solution to keeping them on task.

One after another, the exhausted boys were scraped off their cell floors and were led in utter collapse into the feeding booths. Each booth was small and sported a tiny raised table that was placed flush against the wall. There were no chairs; rather, boys were required to kneel at their places until instructed to sit on the assigned silver circle on the floor. James, now known as #2-273, stood awkwardly in the little space and waited for instructions. His prison time had taught him never to make a first move.

A plastic tray of food was shoved through a slot in the wall and slid onto the table. His stomach pangs gave way to his self-discipline and he eyed #62, seeking permission to eat. The Wellness Team stressed that single-word commands were the only dinner talk that new boys should hear, so #62 uttered her first one. It was the same single-word command that every feeding Trainer said on First Night feeding.

"Kneel," she said.

To her satisfaction, #2-273 lowered his big body and placed his knees into the two slightly padded depressions next to the table. He looked at the food uselessly for a fork but James had spent several years in prison and was released into homelessness so to him, a fork was not required. But #62 waited to see if he would wait for her command.

As he knelt, a green rod rose behind him and pressed into his anus. #62 pressed a button and it sprayed oily liquid between his asscheeks. James's face contorted in surprise, but he did not flinch. His hunger was greater than his humiliation.

The light green plastic food tray had four compartments. Each was filled with an ice-cream size scoop of food: carrots, broccoli, salad and the largest one, a kind of meat mixture he did not recognize. Despite the fact he disliked broccoli and rarely ate salad, it all looked good to him. He was starving.

He reached out with two fingers and pressed a dollop of the meat mixture into his mouth. As he ate, #62 pressed a second button and the anal rod shot upwards into his rectum. It was cold and his ass tightened against the frigid metal. She uttered her second single-word command.

"Carrots," was all she said.

James moved his fingers from the meat concoction, fingered two carrots and pressed them into his mouth. #62 said nothing while James, whose hunger seemed to intensify after swallowing the first bite, kept pressing carrots into his mouth until the tray section was empty.

He moved his hand toward the broccoli but #62 interrupted him.

"Salad," she said.

He quickly reversed course from the broccoli section and began fingering salad into his mouth until that section was as empty as the carrot space. By now he figured it out. He could not choose what to

146

eat until she instructed him what he should eat next. And he had to finish that section before he was allowed to start on the next.

"Meat," she ordered. James used his big fingers to grab meat, shove it in his mouth, chew, swallow and reach for more. He was afraid she would stop him before he was done eating the only food he had seen since last night, so he gobbled whatever she allowed him to eat.

Finally, she said, "Broccoli," and he forced himself to press the green lumps into his mouth. He tried to chew it. He hated broccoli and gulped them down without chewing, all the while trying not to gag.

When he ate it all, she looked at his tray and shook her head from side to side.

"Finish," she said. James noticed a few specs of broccoli remaining on the tray and tried to loosen them, but his fingers were too big and the specs were very small. He managed to push them around on his tray.

He felt the rod press deeper into his ass and it spewed more cold oily liquid inside him. He was growing frantic – afraid of what that rod was spraying into him – and he slid his fingers over and over on the broccoli slot to try to scrape up the remaining bits. His fingers moved faster and faster, all to stop the punishing rod that had risen high inside his dark hole.

The rod started moving in and out of his ass, aided by the oily mess it had pumped into him. His fingers kept sliding and scooping across the tray but could not pick up the remaining broccoli dots. In fear mixed with exhaustion, he picked up the tray and pressed it to his face. His tongue licked every corner of the broccoli section to eat every last bite.

The rod continued its agonizing penetration as he placed the tray back on the low table. In utter defeat, he saw that two bits of broccoli were still stuck on the tray. He did not know that #62 would never reveal that they were permanently affixed to the tray and could never be picked up or licked off.

James' First Night feeding lesson taught him that he could be conquered by two bits of broccoli.

"Done," she said and checked the timer. It took nine minutes and thirty seconds to finish this boy's feeding and she knew that on Second Night, she would have to better that time. The only thing James knew is that his ass was subjected to continuous rod pokings and he hoped against his new reality that she would remove that torture from his backside.

In the other feeding compartments on the train, each new boy was fed in turn and learned what the Trainers' power over them would mean throughout their lives. Feeding lessons taught all new hires how daily meal times would play out every day during their lifelong careers at the Company.

The only hard work Cory ever did was his every-other-day workout in the fanciest gym he could find wherever he was sent on business. He called it a "girl zoo" where he could watch them bend, row, run and stretch. Focusing on their spandex was one of his hidden pleasures and the CEO watched him leer at women, especially blondes, while he did his reps. He gave the women sarcastic names.

Watching the secret surveillance video recorded in the gym and in the locker room made the Intake and Psych teams understand that the only reason Cory worked out was to demean the women he ogled in the gym. Another flagrant character flaw was logged into his record and #54 studied the recommended techniques that she would add to Cory's feeding training.

He named one woman "hippo Hannah" because her build was fuller on the bottom. He slurred another with "Lizard Lisa" because she wagged her tongue when lifting weights and he boasted to the others in the locker room that she would be lucky to be allowed to lick another's woman's pussy while he watched. The men in the locker room laughed and encouraged Cory to give names to different women so they could laugh at his cleverness.

What was detailed as #54's goal was that the new #7-650 would never leer at a woman again and compare her to an animal or think of any woman again as anything other than his superior who was to be obeyed no matter what command she gave. No matter what.

The staff knew that Cory was a fake vegetarian: his restaurant and public meals were always ultra-healthy without the tiniest speck of meat but only when people could see him eat. When he was alone or at home, he gorged on steak, roasts, and ribs. The Psych Team coordinated with Medical for Cory's menu. They knew he would push back but his complaints were of no consequence to them. New boy complaints were predictable. The only question was whether during First Night feeding that he would show his displeasure and what his Trainer would do to correct it.

Crouching by the low table, Cory watched the feeding slot open and a tray was pushed toward him. The first thing he noticed was how small it was and after assessing what occupied each slot, he frowned even though he was incredibly hungry.

Boys do not frown at the Company. They are permitted to have straight lips or open-mouth screams, but there is no frowning or other display of disagreement permitted. #54's task was to teach him that lesson and at the same time, ensure that he consumed his daily allowance of food. Each compartment had to be emptied in less than 10 minutes. That was the Company way.

He fingered the green beans, navy beans, lima beans and white beans. His new diet was to be full of fiber and essential vitamins, plus a dose of tasteless liquid nutrients that would impact his bowels very shortly after ingestion. #54 watched his fingers flick the food around the tray and pressed the button that made the electrified plug start its journey into the boy's ass.

He growled. She ignored him. Then she pressed the button again.

The plug rose deeper into his rectum and spurted what the Medical Team dubbed as *ass grease*. As the plug rose, it oozed lubricant that, when mixed with the lying-in-wait dose of bowel stimulant, forced a boy's bowels to spasm and expel anything inside without warning. They called it *shit on command*. The trainers loved it.

"Eat," #54 said.

Cory turned to stare at her in disbelief. "I want some *real* food," he demanded.

She expected pushback but given Cory's earlier training that made him scream like a madman, she thought it might have taken a little longer. But there was no time like the present, so Cory's submission and acceptance training began right then.

Because Cory's designation ending with zero, he was facing absolute penis denial during his time at the Company. #54 decided to start it right now.

From his crouch, Cory's cock and balls dangled over the depression under the table. If he had behaved and eaten quickly, he would have been allowed to sit and lower his legs into the hole so he could have had a slightly more comfortable meal experience. But privileges like that had to be earned. Instead, his Trainer boxed up his long cock and dark balls into a remote-controlled sleeve with a hard shell made of opaque plastic. It was lined with electrodes. She drew the contraption up between his legs, pulled it hard and attached the cord to his metal belt. When he looked down, he saw no penis, no testicles, nothing! All he saw was a little slit that looked like a horizontal version of a woman's pussy lips. His mind started to explode.

When they are their most vulnerable, refocus them. Prevent episodes of male paralysis and force them to focus on the task at hand.

"Eat," #54 repeated her single-word command.

Cory reluctantly pressed a lima bean into his mouth and swallowed it whole. Not chewing food was an unacceptable behavior at the Company because it displayed a negative reaction and such displays of displeasure were denied to male staffers. #54 tapped a purple button that released a dose of gel that covered his locked-away cock and balls. At first, Cory tried to control his growing growls of pain and tensed his entire body in an effort to not let this evil woman win. He lasted about four seconds.

After tapping the purple button again, Cory's resistance succumbed, and his throat screamed bloody murder. Over and over, he yelled, threatened her, and howled in pain. In a desperate effort to end his suffering, Cory grabbed a handful of beans and shoved them into his mouth. He glugged, tried to chew the hated food, choked a little and finally got them down his throat. Then, #54 touched the lime green button and washed away the pain gel's agony.

Cory realized at that moment that this long, leggy blonde controlled the stabbing pain that attacked his beloved penis and balls.

Psych recommended and the CEO approved that removing pain from time to time taught the male staff that their superiors controlled every aspect of their lives, from pain to simple existence. Pleasure was no longer part of the male staff's experience and stopped being a goal. The Company knew the males would never again enjoy pleasure, but none of the males realized that; instead, they believed that pleasing their superiors every day might one day bring them a little enjoyment. There had to be a break. A little vacation. It was a false hope they hung onto forever.

No Company male deserves remuneration for services. They are mere workers, akin to drone bees. They spend their careers atoning for their lifetime of heinous treatment of women.

Cory's fingers grabbed more beans from the tray, shoved them into his mouth, grabbed more again and repeated the process until the tray was empty. #54 checked the time and noted it into her tablet. Before she released him, she knew he would suffer penis denial so she focused on the cock and balls locked away inside the plastic shell that was hooked between his asscheeks. For good measure, she electrified the box and watched panic overtake him when electrical pulses started to sting his shaft and balls. Fearful what the jabs of current might do to permanently injure his prized manhood, his tear ducts broke through on their own. The big man started crying.

Trainers know to ignore tears merely as physical and emotional reactions that have no place at the Company. To reinforce his feeding lesson, and to make sure #7-560 was given a dose of *shit on command*, she led him to the next round of First Night training, slave toileting.

In an adjacent cubicle, Henry squatted next to the small table and grumbled. He was uncomfortable and hungry and wanted to sit down and eat dinner. But his Trainer, #71, observed him without issuing even a Single-Word Command. He was scrawny with a paunch and was unpleasant to look at but at the Company, only the work that the male staff finished perfectly was important. There were some formerly fat boys who performed at warp speed with expert-level results, so boys' body shapes did not matter because the Company Medical Team always leveled their weight and Esthetics toned them all up by rendering them hairless and looking identical. The trainers and supervisors often could not tell them apart.

That's why the CEO branded the boys on visible areas of their skin as well as under their cocks and installed frenum rings with microchips so they were easy to distinguish. Boys were tracked constantly. None of the staff could hide behind their bald skin and similar shapes.

The Trainers enjoyed Branding day for new hires. Both the new hires as well as those boys who achieved their first rank at the end of their first year were branded in a short ceremony that was broadcast to all divisions in real time. The CEO knew it encouraged the unbranded boys to work harder and faster to earn their own promotions. They coveted getting their own symbols of permanent ownership.

Henry's feeding training was unspectacular. The boy showed all the false bravado that previous boys tried so he might appear in charge of his situation. Like the others, he failed spectacularly. It was a common behavior among Web techs but there was no room for boy-owned control at the Company. With her long, black hair and brown skin, his Trainer, #71, was a visual match for the women Henry brutalized at work. She began training him with the food choices she and Medical set out for him.

He enjoyed causing the mostly Indian female staff he managed discomfort whenever he could, even down to the food ordered for team lunch meetings. He refused their preference for vegetarian choices. #71 and Medical provided his new diet to ensure he would realize how offensive he had been.

His small tray contained individual scoops of tofu roghan ghosht, another slot had one square of dhokla and a dollop of diryani. When it was slid onto the table toward him, he gaped at it in disbelief. #71 ordered him to "Eat." His training was less about slithering his naked body to the table; rather, it was to force him to consume food he spent his working days disdaining.

"I want real food!" he demanded with his false bravado at its peak.

"Kah!" she said as she forced the ass plug into his rectum.

Henry's mouth opened and tried to scream, but she took a finger full of rogan ghosht and forced it in. In that instant, Henry learned that his voice would never be heard, let alone obeyed. He closed his lips only when the Kashmiri chili juices began running down his chin. She ordered him to eat again.

Henry studied his tray hoping to find an inoffensive scoop of anything, but his failure to obey #71's order resulted in the plug dispensing a large dose of fire into his ass. His body responded exactly as #71 knew it would: the skinny new hire bounced uncontrollably up and down on the bench while his cuffed ankles allowed him no escape.

#71 monitored the time it took Henry to put the second bite into his mouth and noted it in her tablet. From the corner of his eye, he saw her take one step toward him and he grabbed the closest scoop and shoved it inside. Boys are not allowed to resist but moreover, they are not permitted to defy a Trainer. She shot another dose of fire into his ass to teach him that he had neither physical nor psychological avoidance while he was employed at the Company.

He ate each additional bite with a sneer. She had the plug shoot bolts of electric shock in his rectum and if he had not been locked onto the bench, Henry would be screaming bloody murder and fallen to the floor. Instead, he just shrieked in place but #71, ignoring his typical boy reaction, just repeated her command, "Kah!"

Tears running down his face, Henry tried to compose himself while trying not to gag. He failed at both. His Trainer entered a few notes into her tablet and when he had managed to get it all down, she allowed him to rise to his knees and begin crawling to his next step in Feeding Training.

He crawled behind her to the next step for all new hires to forced toileting.

Oliver's Trainer had him on his knees in front of the low table that was the locus of his feeding training. Company boys were trained to respect the feeding table and be grateful when they were allowed 10 minutes of feeding time. It was one of their only breaks from a constant stream of new work that had to be completed quickly and perfectly. They were grateful for a small chance to clear their minds. Psych and Medical teams worked short breaks into the boys' rigid schedules so that they did not burn out too quickly. At times, they had to isolate boys who were on the edge of mental breakdowns. They were held in quiet rooms where they received mental health support, learned how to handle their workloads better and were returned to their work. If they had breakdowns in front of co-workers, they were retrained into a new job and assigned to different groups. The CEO's philosophy was that her staff had to perform a variety of jobs quickly and perfectly; so the Company always had fresh workers to perform for her.

#67 nodded and Oliver took that as a silent command to be seated. As he began to rise from his knees, she touched a turquoise button and sharply contracted the ring around his cock. He stared at her curiously and received no hint or reply. He again attempted to stand and walk to the table, and she did it again, longer this time. Oliver feared that his cock and balls would be squeezed so hard that they would atrophy and fall off like a farm animal being castrated, so he fell to his knees again. Breathing hard, he finally remained there, awaiting her to tell him what to do. He was not going to be gelded by this woman over dinner.

Her Asian eyes were like steel and gave off no hint. He remained on his knees and stared at the floor. And waited.

"Kurōru," she said.

He had no idea what that word meant and he hungered for his usual translation programs. If he tried the wrong thing, he was sure that she was going to cut off his cock with that evil bracelet on her wrist. As a network security manager, Oliver was used to having control over every device in his corporation-wide realm and not knowing the specs of that bracelet was driving him crazy.

#67 turned her gaze toward the table and Oliver finally understood that he had to get to the table. But he apparently was not allowed to walk there.

She said, "Akachan."

That was one word Oliver recognized from a Japanese woman who used to work for him until she had a baby and they had to give her maternity leave. Three months! She was gone – and paid – for three months of doing nothing. He had no idea why women would have babies and take a three-month vacation and ruin his department's flow. But he learned that one word from the women whose chattering played in his headset. He often listened in to their conversations mostly to see if they were criticizing him.

She said, "Baby." And he was aghast that she called him a baby. And then it clicked.

She was telling him to crawl like a baby to the table! Who the hell did she think she was? He looked up at her with as much disdain he could muster from his knees. That was when she pressed the turquoise button again and held it down. The contraption that compressed his cock now gripped his testicles in its teeth. And bit down. Hard.

Oliver screamed in pain mixed with outrage. #67 ignored Oliver's petty reaction and glanced at the time it took him to comply so she could record it on her tablet.

Unable to raise himself even to all fours to crawl, he dragged his body toward the table. His naked belly rubbed on the cold tile floor with every small forward movement. Worse, his bagged cock and balls were screaming in pain and his mind was filled with terror that she would cut off the blood supply completely and his penis would shrink to be even smaller than it was and eventually turn black and fall off.

He crept faster.

He finally arrived at the edge of the table and saw her point to the seat. Rolling onto the low bench, he dropped his legs into the pit and waited for his next step to be told to him. As he waited, she raised an electrified plug into his ass and shot *ass grease* into his rectum. Then she added a few drops of *shit on command* and turned her attention to training him how to eat in the Company way.

He felt like his ass was going to explode.

#67 had his food tray delivered and waited a full 60 long seconds before instructing the now-sobbing security engineer to eat. Which he did as fast as he could. He was not sure exactly what he was eating, but he shoved fingerful after fingerful of warm food into his mouth, chewed and swallowed, and then did it again. The entire meal was filled with his silent praying that she let him go to the restroom when he was done.

Never allude to what is next. Make them wonder.
Then take them in a completely different direction.
It keeps them on their toes.

Before #36 led Evan to his feeding training, she leashed his steel belt to her ankle and allowed him to crawl behind her through two narrow train car aisles until they reached the door to the compartment in which she would conduct his instruction. With two "9s" in his name, she knew Evan would resist learning the strict Company feeding processes. Feeding policies were inviolate. His Trainer knew that it was time to make sure Evan learned how feeding worked and behaved properly.

Even though she was bigger and stronger than he was, #36 would never get into a physical altercation with any boy staffer. She knew that he had no idea the CEO might determine him to be untrainable and in very short order, his cock and testicles would live in a jar alongside the other eunuch's organs in a closet off the Medical unit and he would spend his days in the eunuch room, hoping the CEO would buzz for him to perform services for her. The eunuchs were permitted to give her massages, manicures, pedicures, an occasional facial and occasionally, they became the boytoys she used to test new makeup, hairstyles and couture choices. They longed to be the one she dressed up, had make up applied, new hair style wigs and paraded around the trainers' dinner to entertain them all dressed up.

During the long stretches she did not need them, they were passed around and used as lab rats for new anal and hormonal chemicals, test dummies for food additives and forced to perform menial work in support of the landscapers, plumbers and disposal teams. It was worse for them during empty stretches in the eunuch room. Evan had no clue what his number meant. But the recently promoted #36 knew the eunuch room very well. She was not sure how long it would take him to become one of the "used," the penis-less boys who became sex objects for other eunuchs. Those episodes were recorded and played back solely for the CEO's entertainment.

Once in the feeding compartment, #36 turned her back on Evan and used her hip to indicate he should seat himself on the silver ring at the feeding table. He stared at her back incredulously – how dare she use her ass to instruct him? She waited a few seconds and then did two things simultaneously: she bent her shoulder slightly toward the table and shot purple gel into his ass. The shock sent Evan flat onto the floor and thrashing in pain. With her back toward him, it was easy to ignore his writhing and screaming.

She wanted him to sit at the feeding table and be quiet: that was the first step in his feeding training. Psych told her that he would very likely be disrespectful to her and argue with almost every command, so they recommended a new treatment that Medical concocted to address her specific needs with this particular boy. A gray button appeared only on her bracelet during this trek – not the other trainers. It was tested on a few boys the CEO had taken from the wall to be used for this test. Evan would be the first new hire guinea pig and the Teams were eager to find out exactly how it worked with a boy like this.

When his screams subsided to mere gasps, she tapped the dark gray button. The result was sheer madness. #36 turned around to watch.

When Medical tested on the few boys they were given, the reactions were immediate. Each boy responded in almost the same way. They convulsed into near lunacy from pain. Medical showed #36 what the new cock bag did and even she raised an eyebrow at its possibilities.

On command, the new cock bag on Evan's genitals unleashed tiny spikes completely encircling the penis and balls. They stabbed it with dozens of needles at whatever tempo she set. Boys succumbed to its torture fairly quickly and were rendered obedient in short order. But Medical added a second level in the unlikely case it was ever needed.

They showed her how to unleash it and had her practice with a few boys she pulled off the wall. #36 was impressed with how quickly even regular hires morphed from just typical boy lunacy into near psychosis. After testing it on a few boys, she thanked Medical and asked them what the Company would call their invention.

The CEO dubbed it "hell." And that was what everyone called it from then on.

Once she pressed the combination to withdraw the spikes, she gave Evan a single-word command to eat.

It took Evan less five minutes to wolf down the food that appeared in his tray. As she dosed him with *shit on command*, she had him crawl to the slave toilet room at the back of the train and let him anticipate if she would torture him with that evil beast again. What he did not yet realize was that the near madness he just experienced might make the loss of his cock and balls a little less life ending if he failed training. A little.

At the Company, immediately following feeding, every boy was bathroomed. It was the third bathrooming of the day for the male staff and if a boy had not shit on command as was required by Medical during either of the first two, then the third demanded movement of his bowels. Nothing less was acceptable.

After their timed feeding training, the boys were moved as a group to the next step: learning to be bathroomed and to shit on schedule.

Chapter 23

The Company functioned smoothly when the male staff's bowels were emptied every day on the CEO's Company-wide schedule. Psych and Medical worked with Feeding to make sure every staff member shit as scheduled and kept detailed records that included time, quantity, and quality of the stool. The CEO was adamant that no unplanned bowel movements happened because boys' willy-nilly bathrooming might interfere with Company work.

Medical and Feeding examined potential new hires both inside and out before and after they were accepted and started work. With hidden observation equipment and detailed medical histories down to frequency, consistency and type of bowel movements, the teams set up a feeding schedule that promoted regularity so all boys shit when they were told.

They also set up alternatives for those who, in their vernacular, shit too often or not frequently enough. After evaluating the boys' data, they built a blueprint for the different types of boys' bowels in the workforce. They built the shit schedule from that information. There were surprisingly few types of shitters. Most boys fit one profile or another.

Trainers never said "poop." It was a term frowned upon by the CEO and therefore by the Company teams. Trainers who worked directly with boys and new women staffers used the identical single-word command: *shit*.

On the train, new boys were taught that it was not just desirable that they shit at least once a day; rather, they were required to shit simply because that's what they were ordered to do.

After their first dinner training, the new hires were led to the last car of the train and ordered to sit on specially designed toilets. Each seat was smaller than the standard size they were used to and the bowl was significantly lower to the ground than what they knew from their former lives.

As they stared at the little toilets, the curtains that separated them were pulled back. The shit car opened into one big room. Five new hires' jaws dropped at the same time.

Medical advised that squatting with raised feet worked best for boys to re-learn how to shit quickly when it was allowed in their schedules. Each boy reluctantly plunked his ass onto the little low seat and their trainers planted footrests in front of them.

"Feet," one of the trainers said.

James struggled to bend his chest and raise his feet while trying to suck in his too-large gut. Henry planted his feet squarely on the footrest and let his knees drop apart until #71 grabbed his nipples, lifted him upward with them, and stared directly into his shocked face, "Knees!" He snapped his knees together and felt his face redden from yet another dollop of shame.

Cory's height created a challenge for him to sit so low and raise his legs as high as demanded. #54 straddled him and yanked his cock up until his feet were planted squarely on the foot stool. Realizing that she had no empathy for his struggle and he would have to fit into whatever she demanded, Cory sobbed silently into his throat. Oliver was so overwhelmed by the sight of a communal row of toilets that he was unable to move his feet at all, so #67 grabbed a handful of his hair with one hand and his little cock with the other and pulled both up hard. His scream filled the toilet room but none of the trainers paid him the slightest attention. Like all new hires do eventually, he managed to place his feet as instructed. Anything less would get a boy expelled and dropped naked and alone at the nearest train depot.

That left Evan as the last to comply. #36 directed trained her eyes on each movement he made. The boys needed to piss first, and she evaluated which strategy would make every new boy aware that he would obey her command – even to piss or shit – and make him realize that any special status he may have enjoyed in his prior life was gone. It was flushed away like his shit and pee would be very soon.

#71 walked in front of the line of occupied toilets and spoke to all five new hires at once.

"Shit," she said.

Five new hires gaped at her in disbelief. They had to shit on her command? Was even this – the most private function they had – taken away from them now?

The answer to all their questions was "yes." Teaching them how to give up control over every behavior and bodily function was an ongoing task for the trainers. But they always succeeded, or a boy found himself unceremoniously dumped at the nearest station with no ID, money or clothes.

Naked and untrained, just like they came into the world, the CEO said. Nothing more.

Henry opened his mouth to complain but with #71 positioning an electric prod in front of his face, he thought better of it. It was Evan who finally protested out loud.

"I can't pee or defecate with this riff-raff," he started. "I demand a private lavatory."

It took only three seconds according to the video reviewed later that evening for #36 and #71 to tap and point at the newly named #9-908's genital area and blast him in the crotch. It looked like a simple flash of blue light, but Evan's full-throated anguished screams of torture resounded throughout the white-tiled room and informed all the new hires that insolence was not tolerated at the Company.

After seeing what happened to Evan and almost simultaneously, the other four boys grunted and squeezed their sphincters as hard as they could to comply with #71's order to shit on command. For their trainers, even though it was behavior they expected, it was a gratifying moment that they each noted on their training tablets.

The first boy to have successful dump was #3-729 as evidenced by a 'plop' of shit into his little toilet that his Trainer delighted in recording – every first was a positive mark for their personnel files. One after another, each boy expelled shit as instructed and each looked first to #71 and then to their individual trainers to make sure they each knew that the boy had complied as ordered. They were like little children looking to their mommies for approval.

As the stench in the small room grew even more malodorous, the trainers pressed on their stick-on nose guards and turned their eyes to the screaming, trembling boy huddled in a fetal position on the cold tile floor.

"You're done when everyone is done," she said to the group.

The new hires were now stuck on their toilet seats, feet raised on benches and knees held tightly together while inhaling the reeking odor that filled every inch of the room. They all stared at Evan as if their evil-eyed glares could will him to obey the command – one they all had performed – and force him to shit so they could escape the stink and be led – finally – to some much needed sleep.

Evan sucked in his pain and dragged his body back to the little toilet. He rearranged himself on it with his feet raised and knees pressed tightly together in the white-tiled stench-filled room while he considered his options. His mind screamed at him to resist #71's order and retain a shred of his dignity that he believed he was entitled to. But his surroundings offered him no hope that even his bowels still belonged to him – at least at this moment. The scales in his brain tilted heavily toward his inflated self-worth while devising a plan for revenge, but he knew there was a heavy Company finger pressing a button on the other side. It was not time for him to make an escape move. Not yet. Not in the middle of nowhere on this damned train.

He knew that doing exactly what he was being forced to perform was his only solution right now. Especially if he planned to coordinate the other new hires, stupid as some of them seemed to be, to escape from this train trek to hell.

He grunted: once, twice, three times. Finally, the splash in his toilet drew tight smiles from the trainers and an audible sigh of relief from the other boys.

Of course, only the trainers knew that their dinners had been laced with a plant seed that multiplied the stink of the boys' shit. Evan received a larger dose than the others and along with the specific vegetables in his dinner, they reacted nicely together to further humiliate him during his toileting.

The new hires gagged when they inhaled the smell Evan produced and #71 was grateful that the Technical team provided all the trainers with nose guards that nearly obliterated the reeking odor.

The most basic body habits must be redefined to what the Company says: how and when. Males stink. Let them wallow in it.

With that training success under their leather belts, each Trainer led her boy to the adjacent room and inserted a water filled hose into her boy's rectum. Trainers forced the soap to be pumped in and then set the tube to agitate. When the stream that drained out of each boy's ass was clear, the group was marched to their compartments and handed a rough blanket. As soon as the doors were locked, the lights were shut off throughout the training car. First Day was finally over for them.

Chapter 24

There were many skills that all boys were taught and practiced at the Company and the two-day train trek to HQ offered the Trainers adequate time to train the new hires in many first-level requirements. At the end of First Training and after the boys were marched back to their spartan compartments, the Trainers enjoyed a late meal in the Trainers' dining car. Meals were a rare moment for the Trainers where they could relax with their equals.

The CEO dined in her own car with a few hand-picked Trainers while she was always staffed by the necessary boys to handle food preparation, serving and cleanup.

The rest of the Trainers ate together in their own space. Meals were a time that Trainers and staff could speak aloud to each other, make comments, share successes, bemoan failures, and relax – all within strict limits set by the CEO. When the Trainers' dining car was populated, the boys who prepared the food, served, and cleaned it up were outfitted with sound-canceling earphones and special goggles that allowed them to see minimal distances and only straight ahead. They learned how to walk through the dining car taking very small steps, proceeding directly to their destination, and returning to their places on the wall as they waited for their next summons.

All the while, they wore company-issued hard plastic cock-and-ball covers that encased their genitals and were pulled up between their legs, hooked to their ever-present metal waistband in the back. For those who had performed well enough to have had their entire body hair removed by Esthetics, their genital areas appeared like slits and to others, they looked just like tiny nude vaginas.

Nutrition support boys were hosed down – inside and out – before every meal they serviced. Their training took them on a series of steps and only after mastering each step could they hope to serve meals to the Trainers. Only the rare and exceptional workers could ever hope to be a "CEO boy" permitted to attend her private meals.

First, server boys were trained to walk in locked high heels. They could take only wobbly baby steps until they had sufficient practice. The CEO knew that boys with locked heels focused only on their next step and never let their concentration drift from the task at hand. Their stiletto heels were chosen by the CEO for a second purpose. Boys locked in high heels rarely thought about venturing anywhere they were prohibited. You could hear them coming and going; their clicking heels always alerted the supervisors where their boys were walking.

Servant boys who handled food were expertly trained before they were allowed even to see the inside of the Trainers and Supervisors' eating areas at HQ or on the train. Boys practiced high heel walking on the train and until it was perfect, that was where they spent their lives at the Company. Train walking was more difficult and very wobbly as the train headed to or from HQ. It took special practice.

The worst thing a serving boy could do was stumble in his heels when the train was moving. When such a tumble befell a serving boy, Hospitality Training staff took the boy by his red-heeled shoes and dragged the miscreant into the re-training cubicle where he was forced to march around the perimeter for the duration of the train's long trek north. Boys who needed retraining were forced to step repeatedly along the compartment's edges. A Trainer would often change the boy's gait, insisting he skip, run, hop, or take long strides according to the beat of the metronome she played in his headphones. When a boy was in march mode, he often become entertainment for all the women, whether during breakfast, lunch, dinner or late-night snacks. They laughed as he jogged, sashayed, and skipped to the commands that no one could hear but him.

Except for plastic cock covers, serving boys were always kept naked and wore red stilettos locked around their ankles, a condition that was especially amusing to the trainers during a boy's re-training.

As they enjoyed their First Training Day dinner, the Trainers chatted about the new-hire experiences so far. #71 laughed as she related how Henry, when he had not been assigned his number yet, tried to dart away from anal intrusions and how he screamed bloody murder when she zapped the sensitive spots she discovered – and abused – all over his body. #67 made everyone giggle as she spoke of how Oliver really believed a boy was fucking him when it was really a human-feeling fake cock and balls. She had them in stitches when describing how Oliver's sobbing made #41 alert the CEO that he was asking for his mommy. Henry's Trainer, #71, went on about the feral sounds he made gasping for air – air that she controlled – and how she turned the air supply on and off with an unpredictable rhythm. Withholding air helped make him understand that he would never issue another order in his life and would obey even the most incomprehensible commands she – or any other Trainer – issued.

The women ate carefully selected food and drank water over laughter about this crop's training stories. Then they looked at #36, who had yet to share on her First Training experience with the boy formerly called Evan. Hoping for full details about this particular new hire, the women fell silent, sipped their ice water and waited for her report.

The tall, sturdy African American woman took a deep breath. As she spoke, her black skin seemed to shine even more brightly.

"Incredible," she started. "The new tools that Medical set me up with actually pierced him with a single click. It shot antibiotic spray at the same time it pierced. Both nipples in seconds."

The women fidgeted in their seats as excitement over new tools that she was the first to use poured over them. #36 continued.

"But the frenum? Its ass was split wide open and its legs locked apart and I knew there was screaming inside the box even though I could not hear a sound." They all recognized when #36 was in full Trainer mode – she called them "it" instead of "boy." They knew they were in for a treat.

The Trainers leaned in to hear more. She went on, calling Evan "it" repeatedly because her fascination was all about the new tool. The new hire was unimportant and she regarded him only as an "it."

"The button is really expertly designed," she said. "It fits on my thumb so well that I could not misfire, but clamped onto the stretched skin and showed a laser line that showed me when to press the button." She was obviously in awe of the design and the trainers snuggled their thong-split asses and hairless pussy lips into their seats a little harder. They wanted to hear more. They were desperate for more.

"Finally, when I pierced him, I saw a glow from my CEO's icon on my tablet. I knew that #41 was telling her of an incredibly loud scream happening inside the box."

The women pressed their bottoms deeper into their seats and waited for what promised to be an amazing conclusion. #36 did not disappoint.

"She smiled! I saw her smile!"

All the Trainers were squirming their bottoms into the seats and several of them were close to orgasm when their Company training kicked into gear. They stood up almost as a group and one by one grabbed ice cubes from the water pitchers and inserted handfuls into their vaginas to offset their impending orgasms. They dared not break the Company's training rule:

Orgasm is earned and can be awarded only by the CEO. It is a rare prize and is a significant honor. No one experiences orgasm without the CEO's direct order. All climaxes are monitored and recorded for later review.

Chapter 25

Day two of new-hire training began at sun-up for the new boys as all work days would commence for the rest of the lives. With five exhausted new hires sleeping fitfully on their cold concrete floors, their Trainers were already awake. After their morning exercise, the Trainers were showered and groomed by the Esthetics Department trainees who were practicing their techniques and introducing new ones that the CEO wanted evaluated. Trainers never knew what their mornings would bring from Esthetics.

Second Training built on First Training's usual successes in breaking new hires but this particular train trek included a rare occurrence: potential women hires who passed their initial Psych evaluations and whose secret video recordings were reviewed by all the teams and approved by the CEO. If there were failures, they would be dropped off at the next train station with just enough money to get home albeit wearing the same Velcro-closing wraparound light cotton dress they were required to wear when they boarded. And nothing else. The CEO found that expelling them from the train was the easiest way to deal with those who failed to meet her expectations. She never thought about them again.

In the trainers' shower car, the CEO watched the Esthetics team test a new method of preparing the female staff for branding. Only the lowest digits would be honored to wear their CEO's brand at next branding day, but even though it impacted only a few, she wanted them all prepared as if they were selected to wear the Company brand. She disdained worn-out or faded brands and once or twice decided to rebrand a few supervisors because she was not pleased with their brand's pale colors. Supervisors never left the Company until she allowed them to retire at specific Company-built communities.

Today's Trainer group shower started early to provide ample time for a branding demonstration and the CEO watched each monitor carefully to see the entire process from all angles. Only then would she judge the method suitable or reject it outright.

The Trainers had no clue what the trial involved or what its goal was. They accepted whatever was done to them and for them without question and each hungered to be promoted into a lower number that the CEO regarded more highly. When the Esthetics Department had them bend over and grab the rails, they did so without a second thought. As they were marked on their right asscheek, they remained silent. As the hot iron pressed into their flesh, they screamed silently and grabbed the rail tighter.

Each Trainer was thrilled, believing she had been branded. Each of them was wrong. Only the CEO knew that the brand was blank and was being used simply to test skin reaction to new heating methods. The trainers were desperate to see their own – and each other's – brands but feared to move or even wriggle their burning asses until ordered to do so. As the camera visited each asscheek up close, the CEO and the Head of Esthetics conferred. The trainers remained bent over and in searing agony but remained dutifully silent.

Finally, the CEO announced that she had seen enough and told the Esthetics head to bring her the results just before they arrived at the Company headquarters. Dismissing the woman and her entire team, the trainers' asses were sprayed with disinfectant and they were instructed to resume getting ready for Second Training. They did not dare to look at their own asses but when they saw the others' asscheeks with no Company brand, they sadly understood. One fought back tears. But they all vowed that the next branding would be theirs.

Chapter 26

Weeks before this train trek to HQ, a special want ad was posted only for a single Sunday in eight carefully-chosen newspapers and two online job boards that spanned the globe. It ran only once. Replies started pouring into Sybil's inbox before her espresso machine had even warmed up. She was ready to receive applications, but the deluge surprised her. She downloaded spreadsheets of new entries every half hour so she could run them through the complex algorithm that would help the CEO choose the talent pool she wanted for a few very special positions at the Company.

Her algorithms sorted the applicant group into the desired skillsets that the want ad was designed to uncover. With a tap, she could select all the men or women, lawyers, teachers, tech people, recent college graduates, electricians, engineers, or any subset she wanted to evaluate. The CEO was especially specific that separating and merging skills was the crux of the formula that would populate the new worker set she was creating at the Company.

Sybil had recently been raised in rank to #34 and reported more directly to the CEO. She loved seeing her number flash on the call board when the CEO needed an important job done. In her prior life, Sybil worked for a company with more than 8,000 employees worldwide until that special day she answered a different kind of online want ad that promised she would get a new lifestyle in exchange for a five-year work commitment. After her nine years at the Company, Sybil could not imagine working anywhere – or doing anything – else.

The CEO had her trained and made sure Sybil grew her skills. And now her task was to find three very special women applicants to become Trainers for a special group of new hires. Women hires were rare at the Company and they required specific personalities and unique sets of skills. Sybil, who rarely even thought about her former name because she identified herself now as #34, crunched the data to put together women with the capabilities that would serve the CEO brilliantly for the new division and new type of Trainers who would oversee the male workers who were to staff it.

All the trainers learned how to deal with a variety of male egos and backgrounds but the new women were going to be groomed not just to train new hires; rather, they would become the pièce de resistance in the CEO's corral. She knew what characteristics and talents the CEO wanted in the new females, but she did not understand why these criteria were so important. She also knew her job was to find what the CEO wanted and not concern herself with "why." When assigning her this job, the CEO told her directly,

Present new hire candidates with what they despise and make them subservient to it. They will submit to what they hated. Then they will be mine.

With her spreadsheets sorting data by height and weight, personality traits and bra size, #34 gleaned eight possible candidates for further testing and an intense secret background research package. The CEO never asked a candidate if she wanted to be videotaped. Rather, she sent an experienced team to record private scenes, tap conversations and observe the candidates' home grooming, showering, bathroom and feeding habits.

No one was ever invited to an interview without first having been completely analyzed by the Company Psych Team through clandestine recordings. Photography was too old-school for the CEO's needs. She wanted to see potential hires in action when evaluating them for possible roles as new Trainers. She also required full-body visuals in addition to psych tests.

In several cases in prior years, the CEO sent job applicants to the want-ad responders' places of business to be interviewed by them if they were the hiring manager. In other situations, she sent undercover "parents" to a school to observe a teacher. In still others, Company spies could be IT tech support, medical insurance consultants and even once, a catering team that produced surprisingly intimate results. Once they applied, the CEO owned their lives.

Gathering the pre-interview team, #34 outlined the results that the CEO expected them to find out and gave them detailed instructions.

"Take high quality video of body structure, clothing and underwear, interactions with their superior and inferior women and men, feeding routines, sleeping habits, toileting and, of course, interactive sex and masturbation episodes."

The team studied the half-page list of requirements and committed them to memory. No team traveled with any Company identifying information except the IDs and credit cards created for them. With an experienced team like this one, it took only a few hours before they became the personas that were constructed for them.

They were sent in teams of two to six cities to gather information about the applicants that #34 had selected and that the CEO approved as finalists. She needed only three new females, but they had to be the best of the best, so she ordered evaluations of the top eight. Only #34 knew what was on the CEO's most-wanted list. She never shared that with the teams in the field so they would gather unbiased data and especially complete media.

Unbeknownst to the applicants, the Company's surveillance began within hours of #34's spreadsheet sorting. Teams infiltrated homes and workplaces, installed cameras and microphones, set up fraudulent business meetings and took on the roles of common servicers like cable installers, food delivery staff and spa guests. Within just few hours, recording began.

Women who applied were tracked 24 hours a day and their habits and interactions recorded. Every few hours, #34 downloaded video and audio to review, passing along those that best reflected the CEO's list of requirements. Whether the women passed or failed did not matter. The CEO studied all of them.

Two unusual requirements stood out to #34 from the CEO's list: bra size and masturbation habits. Of course, there were dozens of other factors, but her instructions clearly stated she required full breast video and analyses of their self-sex episodes including tools, positions, and sounds. #34 never questioned her CEO's specifications but at times she wondered what the new position would eventually entail.

The teams' surveillance eliminated one applicant quickly and her information was deleted from the Company files. Her bra size was false. She was much smaller-breasted than she entered on the application and breast size was a big factor on the CEO's demands. The other five were analyzed more diligently with more intimate video that focused on their breasts and pussies during masturbation. The team posed as spa guests and chatted with the unknowing women bringing up confidential details regarding waxing and how they used vibrators that spa visitors were eager to share. Those recordings usually produced better video for #34 to scrutinize and add to the CEO's video reel. Women acting as food deliverers surreptitiously added chemicals to boost the applicants' sexual drive to the applicants' dinners to score higher-quality video for the CEO's review.

The one woman who ordered the odd combination of shrimp and chocolate syrup with her grocery delivery intrigued the Company shopper. When watching the live feed later that evening, she watched the woman dress in a see-through lavender negligee and eat shrimp and a chocolate milkshake while vibrating herself almost to the point of orgasm. Each time she groaned with an impending climax, she put down the vibrator and gorged on more shrimp. The process repeated itself until the woman downed the milkshake, rammed a dildo into her pussy and held the vibrator on her clitoris until the unseen observer had to lower her earphones' volume to deal with the woman's ensuing scream.

That made excellent post-dinner video for the CEO who laughed through the entire episode.

Finally, the CEO determined she had enough footage and invited five women to be interviewed for the three new positions. They were contacted electronically and signed their five-year commitments. The teams delivered small boxes to each one's home and rang the bell remotely after they had left the visible area. Applicants were told to read the instructions and comply with all of them in order. Any who differed from the rules were eliminated on the spot and never heard from the Company again.

After they complied with the instructions, a black SUV with tinted windows picked up each woman and delivered her to the transportation that would take them to the train. After each woman climbed into the SUV, she was inspected by an Intake team member to make sure she was wearing only the provided wrap-around light cotton dress and sandals. They pulled the single Velcro clasp that held it shut and removed the sundress. The Intake team member looked at every inch of skin and lifted every fold to make sure the women were completely naked. When that inspection was done, each said the same single command, "Re-dress."

Drivers took their wallets, phones and passports so the women carried nothing during the silent car ride. They were each driven to a nearby private airport and one team member flew with each applicant. All five were met by the Transport team and delivered quickly to the train. The entire Intake process was handled in total silence.

The women, clad in identical wrap-around strapless cotton dresses held closed with a single Velcro patch, boarded the train. To her trained eye, #34 saw that none of them seemed to be trembling – that would have eliminated them on the spot, and they would be handed travel vouchers to return to their home cities. Their identification would be sent a few days later and everything about them would be deleted permanently from Company records.

They were ushered up the three train steps one by one in complete silence. They were all assigned a bare compartment that served all their needed functions: testing, feeding, toileting and Company evaluation. The CEO preferred keeping female candidates in a single cell and limit their interaction with trainers and staff. How they were eventually introduced to the Company and later, to new boy hires, was completely controlled.

The CEO enjoyed First Meetings with new women. She had the women, who were totally unaware of what would happen next, stripped of their small carry-on with their IDs that had been returned to them before boarding. That left them wearing only one thin layer of cotton – all that separated them from complete nakedness. The applicants were secured in a cell in a female training car on a moving train.

Those applicants that survived First Meetings often graduated to prized jobs in the Company. They just did not know what the possibilities were yet. The ones who did not make it were dropped off at the nearest train station wearing only a Velcro-closed sundress and sandals and holding a ticket voucher.

On her signal, #41 opened the compartment doors where focused lighting made sure the women could see nothing in front of them, but the CEO and her staff could study the women under bright spotlights. The cell walls were drawn back and the applicants were lined up side-to-side. #47 stepped into the compartment and told each woman to step forward and step into pairs of floor depressions. She locked metal restraints around each ankle so the women were stationary. The small width of the room forced them to be jammed shoulder to shoulder. Noise-cancelling headphones covered their ears. Other than smell, none of their other senses would do them any good where they were now.

On cue, #41 spoke quietly into their ears.

"Grip the overhead rings," she said. #58 studied her screen to make sure the women, who she would likely be instructed to oversee and train, complied.

The CEO rose and proceeded to her favorite task in bringing new women to her fold. She gripped the elastic band on the flimsy dress of the applicant standing the farthest to the right and lowered it, exposing the woman's breasts. The entire training cadre viewed and evaluated them. The Wellness team took notes about size and shape; the Esthetics Department studied hair; the Training staff evaluated nipple size. Then #35, once known as Emma a long time ago, zoomed into the cell to assess what size needle would be required for each one's piercing.

The CEO left those specifics to her teams. What she wanted to evaluate for herself was the size and sturdiness of their bosoms. She lifted each breast and juggled it. She squeezed it and dropped it to let it sag. She pinched nipples and observed reactions. Most of all, she enjoyed pressing them together to determine their ability to smother a boy's face when pressed into them. Satisfied with the first set of breasts, she moved to the next and performed her inspection again.

Each woman's reactions were recorded by #41 and #47 for later review. The CEO wanted to see for herself if any of the new woman applicant was at all aroused by her exceptionally sexual touching. The masturbation videos previously revealed which women were pussy-firsters (rarely interesting to the CEO) and which went for their breasts for orgasm – even before they used their vibrators. One of her best Trainers was an older woman who achieved orgasm only with breast stimulation and the CEO spent many sessions watching her writhe merely from a bound boy staffer's sucking her teat.

It was time to take the new females' interviews to Phase Two.

Chapter 27

Five blindfolded women stood with their breasts hanging out under bright lights as the CEO moved to the next step in evaluating which three she might keep. With their senses receiving no input and their ears hearing nothing except what #41 said into their earphones according to the CEO's directions, several were becoming alarmed at what was happening.

They had been in the hands of the Company on the train for only two hours.

Most women applicants were startled and humiliated at this point. In prior applicant interviews, some women tried to talk, ask questions, and even expected answers. Some objected. Others screamed complaints. Over time, the Intake team recognized most of those personality types and excluded them. Today's five potential new hires stood quietly as their breasts were again inspected, pinched, juggled, tossed, and then dropped according to the CEO's desires.

The CEO returned to her gliding chair and nodded to #34 as if to say, "Job well done." In response, #34 dropped to her knees and bowed all the way to the floor toward her CEO in appreciation.

"Next," the CEO instructed the staff.

Second on the Intake list was a closer look at the women's bellies, pussies and asses. The CEO had specified in #34's instructions that she must provide women with rotund, sagging bellies and pussies with big lips. Trainers lifted the back of the applicants' dresses and tucked them into the elastic band, so their tops and bottoms were exposed. Except for the sundresses that were now tucked into a form that looked more like cloth belt above their waists, the women were naked.

People who are forcibly stripped will instinctively press their legs together to hide their genitalia. But the applicants' feet were locked wide apart and their wrists were manacled to the wall handles so they were exposed and on-display like animals in a zoo. It was important that all staffers scrutinize their bodies because the selected females would become Company property. So would their skills and talents. It was all Company property.

A wide band was stretched under their bulging bellies and lifted. With their overhangs lifted, the staff could see five pussies very clearly and brilliantly lighted.

Using an electronic tool designed by Training in conjunction with Esthetics, trainers-in-training used large tongs to lock onto each pussy lip and pull them apart so Medical could inspect for rate of use and possible damage and take a first-day reaction reading. As the CEO conferred with her trainers and issued initial notes, Esthetics peered at each clitoris and rated them for reaction to a current that they zapped on each one. Both physical and psychological reactions were recorded.

Especially interesting to the Intake group was evaluating each woman's full body jerk when her clitoris was stimulated. The one standing farthest to the left was particularly entertaining to them with her shriek of pleasure when zapped. Two of them humped air as if begging for more and one began circling her hips. But it was the last one that provided the most entertainment.

That one, who easily had the biggest breasts of the group, literally drooled from her vagina when zapped. #41 repeated it to make sure what she saw really happened. Catching the CEO's eye, she nodded as if to say, "We've got another one." The CEO's return nod was all the affirmation that #41 needed.

With a baseline established, the CEO moved to phase three.

Platforms whirred into place under the women's asses and both their ankle and wrist restraints rose to force their legs apart father and raise their pussies. Their heads hung backwards and their arms were lowered. The only thing the CEO wanted to see during this phase were pussies unobscured by hairy labia or big bellies. Spotlights were positioned to illuminate them fully.

To prevent unnecessary noisemaking, the Trainers stuffed their mouths with red ball gags.

Nothing that boy staffers utter and nothing applicants say is important or will be heeded.

The CEO rose from her gliding chair and approached the farthest-right applicant in the display. She peered closely at her open pussy. Her Trainers showed her the baseline stimulation readings and she gripped her personal evaluation tool to check their accuracy. Placing the pin-point tip on the woman's clitoris, she worked it up and down while delivering a set level of electric shots that she lowered and raised at whim. The Wellness team determined which electrical levels would excite a clit and which levels could lead to orgasm. The CEO modulated the current just north of excitement and always south of orgasm.

Staffers were not allowed to orgasm at the Company except when the CEO specifically used one to demonstrate a specific training technique and on rare occasions to amuse herself while observing an individual or team orgasm together. She ensured that males never experienced orgasm, although she might move them toward it and then suddenly deny it. It kept her boys on their toes. As for women, orgasms had to be earned and were all done under her watchful eye.

The applicant being stimulated at that moment had no control over her body's reactions. Phase Two produced the most accurate electrical level that the individual needed for "just under orgasm" and it was carefully recorded so a higher level would never be applied. Taking staff to the edge of coming and then dropping them down quickly was one of her most effective and favorite training techniques. She enjoyed knowing they were screaming for more while she turned and walked away.

Each applicant in turn was stimulated with a mix of pin-point pain and electrical pleasure. There was no Trainer skilled enough to perform this task and the CEO was the sole user of the "O-wand," as the teams dubbed it for their Owner.

One pussy after another was tested and each woman was brought to the edge of orgasm only to be denied relief. Time and time again, the CEO took them to an edge and then walked away to torture the next applicant in line. Finally, #34 presented her with the charts illustrating the range of electrical allowance she would use to torture these women toward the moment of completion, only to remove it and bring the woman to that apex again. And again.

It was time to move to Phase Three of new applicant intake.

Chapter 28

As the women's' feet were lowered and locked, knees spread and their hands chained to the cell walls, Trainers gathered the five new hires to begin Second Day training. A brilliant strategy devised by the CEO to measure both new women hires' and new males' appropriateness for the Company simultaneously, this exercise showed how much new hires were able to use any of their expertise in unfamiliar situations. It also exposed which boys had no useful talents to serve women. Many personality traits would be ticked off the CEO's list during this phase and that provided crucial information about both new women and new males' potential as Company employees.

The new boys began Second Training by being mass toileted, scrubbed and delivered wearing blindfolds to the training car where they knelt on small platforms in front of each new female applicant. The boys' wrists were locked behind their backs and their ears covered with headsets into which they would be issued instructions. One metal band that hung from shoulder straps circled their chests. Jaw expanders were locked into their now-gaping mouths.

The tiny platforms that held kneeling, naked new hires moved both horizontally toward the women and vertically, so the boys' open mouths were pressed against the new female recruits' huge bosoms. Directions were sent to the boys' ears from #41's microphone.

"Tongue," #41 intoned. "The first boy to bring the breast to orgasm will be rewarded." She added, "Those who fail will be punished." She let her words sink in before ordering, "Start!"

Each boy knelt imprisoned with his stretched jaws pressed firmly against a huge breast with only his tongue able to move. Locked in place with breast flesh overfilling their mouths, the startled boys tried to understand what they were supposed to do, let alone how to begin working on the task. But the threat of punishment overcame their confusion. For some of these boys, intentionally bringing a woman to orgasm was outside of anything they had done before.

Cory, now named #7-650, started first and licked the nipple gently with his tongue. His Trainer, #54, was reminded every time she glanced at his numeric name that the "7" meant he required close supervision. And direction. From behind his kneeling frame, she reached around and attached tight clamps on his nipples. As an immediate pain reflex, he tried to bite down. The breast's owner made a noticeable noise that sounded like something between a small groan of pain and a tiny moan of pleasure. Her Intake Trainer, #94, noted it on her tablet and nodded at #54 to have the boy increase the pressure.

#54 tightened the nipple clamp's teeth.

With his tongue now licking wildly, Cory was learning that he had to dispose of his usual sex games where he pretended to satisfy a woman. To win – to avoid punishment – he needed to make this breast's owner scream louder and expel more excited noises, even though he could not see or hear her react. After First Day training, he knew that he would do almost anything to avoid punishment. He was about to learn the most important understanding of the Company's training regimen: that he would do absolutely anything and everything demanded of him for the rest of his life, just to avoid punishment.

For her part, the new woman, temporarily dubbed #101, threw her head back in growing pleasure. She tried to spread her legs, a movement noted by #94. Grasping his head with both hands, #54 pulled Cory's mouth away from the nipple, pulled it to the left, and stuffed #101's other breast in his mouth. Now Cory's focus was moved to the other bosom and he had to start again pleasing her again from scratch. His Trainer noticed that the boy obviously did not know how to start.

Tired of waiting for him to try something new, #54 tethered Cory's testicles in a plastic tie that held a net bag and she secured it around the balls. With a bracelet button press, she saturated his cock and balls with a chemical irritant. As it took effect, he forgot about the breast in his mouth while his body humped uncontrollably in a useless effort to escape the horrid gel. But the chest restraint kept him locked in place and the only motion his body could do was lick with his tongue while his cock and balls felt like they were burning in hell.

The tall man morphed into a wildly licking mass of dark brown flesh and #54 noted exactly how much time it took him to get there. Losing his mind's control and acting purely with visceral physical reactions was where he would spend the rest of his life working for the Company and pleasing – when required – any deserving Trainers. Only those boys who could shed their old male-learned barriers would become Company workers. And #54 would not tolerate a failure on her record.

The big-breasted woman, secured by her ankles, chest band and head encased in a sensory deprivation box that the CEO could see into on her screens, started moaning in a peculiar rhythm. Cory heard nothing but felt her small hip gyrations as each breast pressed closer to his face. He remembered the warning, "failure = punishment." His tongue started licking ferociously and he rubbed her breast against his teeth to simulate chewing. #101's groans grew but Cory heard nothing and could not tell if his efforts were accomplishing anything at all. #54 was desperate to own the winning boy in this training exercise, so she added a second dose to his testicles and cock, this time the chemical known – and feared – around the Company as *fire*. It seemed the best choice for this exercise, #54 believed.

He screeched bloody murder.

But somehow, he managed to almost chew and rapidly tongue the breast in his mouth harder and faster. The #101 on the training platform swung her hips as far as she could and tried to spread her legs again. The scene filled #54's notes and would show the speed at which the boy crossed over into providing real pleasure for a woman, as opposed to his habit of giving as little attention as possible to his dates – just enough for them in order for him to finish – and leave every one of them wanting more.

#7-650's new designation numbers, issued by the Trainers and approved by the CEO, showed that he could perform to expectations for some of the required categories, but the "6" in his name told the Trainers that he was to be punished daily to remind him what he had to overcome and what his lifetime learning experience would be going forward. Even if he performed decently today, he needed daily punishment to keep him well trained. #54 used another bracelet button and released what the Training Team called *hysteria*, a chemical that usually drove boys to the floor, writhing in agony and deafening anyone nearby with primal screams of agony. #54 had not used it yet on a new hire, but she knew how it worked and about how long it would last. She had used it successfully before.

A single dose was applied to his cock and balls and Cory promptly devolved into insanity. Ignoring his screaming and wailing, his Trainer checked her tablet to see what was next on Second Day training for this boy.

The only requirement left for him to learn in this session was to bring the owner of the breast in his mouth to physical orgasm. She set a timer so the process could be recorded in her tablet and ignored the boy's descent into senselessness for what she figured would last about 30 more seconds.

The CEO noted the Trainer's achievement and shifted her focus to the next boy in line.

This boy had been named #6-437 and his Trainer, #67, ran a mental checklist that reminded her that this boy was classified as "Punish daily" worker. He was a known malingerer. The former IT security engineer was locked on his knees with his jaws spread open when #67 adjusted the platform's height so his mouth was even with the giant jiggling breast that was mere inches from his face. When she was satisfied with his position, she moved the platform forward so the big breast was pushed fully into his open mouth.

Oliver choked and gagged when his stretched lips were filled with #102's big bosom. #67 noted his failure to start licking immediately when a woman's body position clearly indicated what he was supposed to do. She smeared a dab of fire gel on his nipples and then added teethed clips. Within seconds, Oliver was trying to scream but his separated jaws and bosom-filled mouth let him make no sound louder than a deep moan. Trainers, especially those with #67's experience, had no time for boys' noises, so she wrapped his balls in a net bag and pulled the tie shut. Then she dosed his sensitive skin with one of the Medical Team's more recent additions to the Trainers' tools. She pressed a purple button on her bracelet. It was her first time using the new *fire* and this boy's reaction would give her useful test results.

She watched his face contort into what the Medical Team promised would be a silent scream of pure torment. Had he been unchained, Oliver would have run around his cell, shrieking in pain, trying to tear off the offending testicle bag or press his whole package into a wall or even the floor, all in a useless attempt to relieve his cock and ball agony. #67 practiced meditation on the rare times she received punishment, but this boy had none of her contemplative ability. After all, she worked hard on that so she could use it when she was forced to cope with pure pain as the daily experience of her own training.

The boy was, quite figuratively, running around insanely in his head while his body remained immobile on the small platform on which he was kneeling with a fat breast pushed into his mouth.

What Oliver did not know was that the *fire* chemical treatment would become part of his routine at the Company. The "6" in his designation made him one of many who experienced "punish daily" exercises. He could never be convinced at this early stage in his training, that soon he would anticipate happily to his own daily torture.

#67 was fed up with his failure to start performing. She pushed the boy's face deeper into the breast and cut off his oxygen so he could focus on doing his job. When she released it for a moment, Oliver gasped and finally remembered the breast, his tongue, and his job. He started licking.

Dissatisfied with how long it took this boy to begin, his Trainer drilled a spark rod into his ass. The force of insertion made #6-437's tongue and teeth work harder, and his Trainer noted this small accomplishment on her tablet. She would recommend that his boy's career training would include testicle and penis torture combined with ass penetration. That suggestion would become a part of the lifelong plan to make Oliver a useful Company employee.

The CEO shifted her view to the next monitor.

It was James, to be known as #2-273, who showed some promise in this training exercise. His Trainer, #62, sported her own large breasts and ample belly, very similar in size and shape to the woman whose bosom was currently forced into James's mouth. He knelt quietly on his small platform with his head down as the platform level was adjusted. As soon as the breast touched his spread lips, he sucked it in. Then he used that same sucking technique to pull more of it in more deeply. This unusual tactic made #55 listen for the woman's reaction and her initial moan proved that she was reacting as predicted.

The boy's cheeks tightened and loosened as he worked the bosom in and out of his mouth. When it was out, he licked it. When it was in, he sucked down on it. #55 had not seen that method used by a boy in several treks on the train, so she noted it on her tablet. Then he expanded his service without any encouragement by searching for the second breast with his lips. When he found it, he sucked both nipples and licked them rapidly.

The female, designated #103 during her audition for a job at the Company, was locked in her own new-female training position. She moaned loudly, and #41 heard it clearly in her headset. She nodded at #62 who sensed that her boy might provide her a victory in this training session and #41 also wanted that success on her own record. It was time to speed things up.

She drew a genital bag around his cock and balls and tied it. She noticed the boy's cock tip was drooling and she knew what to do with this unacceptable behavior. By pressing a green button on her bracelet, she shot a hit of icy chemicals into the bag. This was a useful reminder for every boy that a boy's focus must be on the woman he was serving. The ice hit its mark and James shot back in shock as far as his chains allowed. He took a big breath and then pressed his face deeply into the woman's bosom again. Straining against his jaw lock, he tried to chew the nipples, while sucking and tonguing #103's breast at the same time.

James had been trained in prison to do exactly what he was forced to do and he probably sucked not just a few cocks, a chore that convicted rapists are often forced to perform. #41 sensed a win in this exercise and she was eager to get it on her own record.

The female focus of his frenzied licking and sucking shook violently. The woman's cries were shared briefly by #41 who allowed them to play for a few moments on the speakers. #62 could feel her victory almost in hand and she continued her assault on James by setting off freezing puffs into his net bag.

The CEO was briefly amused by the freeze/shake choreography taking place on that platform and moved her attention to the next woman in line.

Henry, the next boy in the lineup of platforms had been designated #3-729. His Trainer read up on his stubbornness and disrespect toward women in what was now his previous life. He would need constant re-checks to ensure he was not simply pretending to respect the Company women. The CEO would send any play-actor or malingerer off the train immediately at the next available stop, no matter how desolate it might be. She left them there naked, with no funds or ID, and let each of the failures fend for himself. #71 did not want that indignity to smudge her record, so she was determined to force Henry to pass this test.

The female, temporarily numbered #104, was bolted securely in front of Henry. She sported a big bush of black pubic hair and several long hairs growing out of her nipples. The CEO would – if this one was accepted – assign her immediately to the Esthetics Department to undergo full body hair removal. The CEO believed that all new Company employees should start their new careers completely naked, and that included every hair on their bodies, including their heads. She would routinely have them sent to Esthetics to be waxed and shorn into complete hairlessness until she deemed them worthy of the right to grow any head hair. There was no head hair for women at the Company until it was earned, although boys were always kept hairless from head to toe. From time to time, those women who earned successes were allowed only a few pubic hairs that the CEO had styled and dyed to her liking.

#71 used a technique she developed to force Henry to move past his disrespect and stubbornness. She lowered his platform so his face was even with the woman's black bushy pussy. She pressed his face into it and out of it, then in and out again. His head, mouth and lips had become nothing more than another one of his Trainer's tools to satisfy a woman and his face became the dildo she used to move #104 toward orgasm.

First, she fucked the potential Trainer's pussy with #3-729's nose. The clitoris responded, as evidenced by #41's nod that said #104 was, at the least, moaning.

The platform inched upward so the breast was now ready for Henry's drooling mouth. Then it was moved forward to force the bosom between his spread jaws. With a deft motion, #71 attached and tightened the net bag around his puny cock and tiny balls before pressing her bracelet's yellow button that spread the tool they called *shrink*. That added a spray of something wet on his skimpy package before it dried almost instantly and tightened dramatically.

Henry felt the first tug of tension and then rapid tightening as his cock and balls were compacted as if in a vise. He struggled to raise and lower his torso, but his chains held him in place. #71 added sharp-toothed nipple clamps and smiled as the boy attempted to scream. Henry felt his cock and balls being crushed into nothingness and his nipples screeched with pain.

#71 pressed his head deeper into the breast to remind him exactly what he was there to do. His tongue began licking mildly and his Trainer spurted more *shrink* onto his genitals. The breast muffled

Henry's attempt at screaming and he tried to bite and chew, always failing against the jaw spreader's grip. As part of his new designation, he was known to be stubborn and required constant retraining, so #71 pressed his face in so deeply that she cut off his air supply.

Henry freaked out completely and the observers were always amused at chained bodies as they tried to become hysterical. They failed all the time. In fact, if you did not know his oxygen had been cut off, you would assume the trainee was simply performing the breast licking and fucking exercise using his head. Until Henry began completing his assignment with gusto, his Trainer kept his face where it was. Boys at the Company had to learn that they ate, drank, worked, slept and even breathed when the Company saw fit.

Finally, Henry's tongue began moving so #71 allowed him to draw in a breath or two. He licked harder and #71 awarded him two short breaths. It took 3 tries before he understood. Only then did she allow him to breathe.

The CEO moved her attention to the last monitor.

The final boy in line was Evan, newly named #9-908. Trainers were not given many "9" boys on the train. The CEO accepted very few of them. If she needed their skills, she would allow one on rare occasions but they always sported an "8" in their number, a reminder to everyone at the Company that unless this boy learned his place and performed exceptionally well, that its penis and balls would be lopped off and the boy would be housed in a special wing with other eunuchs who were used from time to time by the CEO for entertainment and her own personal pleasures.

The trainers remembered the time they were allowed to witness the CEO's use of a few of the cockless workers. They never had numbered designations; rather, they were referred to as "8." Cockless males were mostly invisible at the Company. She stripped them of everything from hair to cock and moved them to a lifelong reality and used them for her occasional personal needs. Eunuchs were not human to the CEO.

When she was done using them, the CEO gave them to Company staff who had earned privileges. The Wellness, Training and Esthetics staffers were allowed to enjoy being pampered by the 8's who daintily performed foot and full-body massages, pedicures, pussy licking or whatever they had earned. The best part about them was they wanted – and got – nothing in return.

Eunuchs were a silent part of the Company and were never allowed to speak. The CEO liked them in silence so that became their life's work. If Evan were trainable, he would join the workforce. If not, he would join the 8's and remain invisible forever. He would lose the designation the Trainers gave him and become an object referred to as an "8." But the new boys did not know about the role of 8's at the Company. They would find out more about them after Second Day training when they arrived at HQ.

#36 stood behind the kneeling Evan and waited for her cue. With their prior research of Evan's peccadillos and likely training difficulty, each step in his trek on the train was carefully mapped out. In fact, they planned alternatives in the unlikely case his resistance interfered with any other new hire's training. As his Trainer aligned his platform with the potential new female's giant bosom, Evan fidgeted on his knees.

When instructed, #36 moved the platform forward so Evan's spread jaws were stuffed with a huge nipple and as much of #105's breast as #36 could shove in. He gagged from the bosom's smothering fullness. While he choked, the Trainer wrapped his cock and balls in a training bag. Between gurgling and screaming from the cock bag incarcerating his prized organs, Evan had forgotten the task he had been assigned.

She moved his little platform forward and back to remind him he was supposed to be attending to the flesh in his mouth. He was drooling and could not get away from the breast overflowing his jaws. #36 felt him start to panic. Grabbing a handful of his thinning hair, she jerked his head backward and stared into his sightless eyes.

"Tongue!" she said. #41 relayed her order into Evan's headphones.

His throat gagged; his cheeks trembled. He fought against complying and teetered on the edge of submitting to the breast that filled his mouth. In a brief instant that the CEO saw on her monitor, she saw his body sag slightly. And she knew he had just surrendered.

She knew the boy was hers. He just did not know it yet.

Chapter 29

Training Henry to Work

Disappointed at not being branded earlier that morning and used only as test subjects, the Trainers dutifully donned their work clothes to begin the next phase of Second Day Training, one that they dubbed "Work Skills." Once new hires were finished being used as part of the females' auditions and were themselves broken in more deeply by the experience, the next thing they needed to understand was exactly what they would be doing for the Company every day for the rest of their lives. The Company workforce had specific skillsets and each new hire had to learn his job, how he would do it and what training he needed to perform perfectly.

There was no "mediocre" Company work product. Boys were taught that they did not clock out at 5pm and go home for dinner or out for drinks. Their lives were their careers – and vice versa. They had to work perfectly and turn in perfect work every day.

Five naked new hires were leashed by their Trainers and marched in a line to the Work Skills car. Each was led into a cubicle with walls on 3 sides. The open side faced their Trainer as well as multiple cameras that provided the CEO's live feed. Each boy had headphones buckled under his chin so the only sounds he heard would come directly from his Trainers.

The new hires were plunked unceremoniously on low curved seats that forced them to squat with their knees spread to maintain balance. Similar to the work chairs at the Company, this seated position was found to produce the fastest and most accurate work because boys were prohibited from standing until their assignment was completed and their work product as evaluated to be perfect on the Company's rating scale. They learned to work fast and accurately just to relieve the torture that their work seats inflicted on them.

Henry and Oliver, now known as #3-729 and #6-437 respectively, faced monitors and keyboards that would be the primary tools of their new careers. Each was loaded with the software programs that were like those used at the Company, but each was a different test of how they would approach their jobs at the Company every day. Careful programming of the exercises included evaluating their skill levels but mostly trained them how they would start their workdays and when their work would be considered finished. They needed to learn the Company way of working.

Henry's test program demanded that he design an interactive form to use on the Company intranet through which the Esthetics Department would evaluate a potential new technique. The assignment was clear: develop a series of questions with conditional logic that provided information that the team needed to evaluate their results. But the Company never explains to a new hire the exact nature of the test. The task was only partially about the form; the real test was how quickly Henry, whose #3 prefix indicated he required constant re-checking, adapted to this new style of work.

#71 read the assignment into Henry's headset and then instructed him to nod if he understood. Groggy from the previous day's First Training and with only fitful sleep on a concrete floor, Henry nodded. He stared at the screen for a few moments before his web skills kicked in and his fingers began typing. Forms were not new to him and building surveys was a particular talent of his. Unbeknownst to #3-729, his Trainer was well aware of this boy's strong – and weak – suits. They would both be put to the test in this exercise.

Henry tried to focus on the monitor while nudging his ass into the backless seat. He added form fields and well-tested question formats but realized he was missing the most important piece of data: what product was being surveyed? Pushing down his dislike of reporting to women supervisors, he asked #71 that obvious question.

"What are we measuring?" he asked.

His Trainer did not supply an answer quick enough for him, so he asked again. By this time, #71 had broken into a grin and tapped her tablet to enter the boy's failure to grasp the obvious.

Because she was standing under special lighting, he never saw the small grin on her face. He tried again with the same useless results and his anger rose. Damned if he were going to ask again, Henry replaced the product name with code that could be easily filled in when the mystery noun was ultimately revealed. He continued building the form until it contained the usual 10 questions and a single paragraph text box.

Pay attention to how many times they repeat the same actions before realizing they get the same failure each time.

Believing he was finished with the assignment, the boy decided to stand up and relieve his aching ass. He managed to rise about an inch before the metal hook that attached itself to his steel chest belt prevented any vertical movement.

"What the hell?" he asked aloud as he plopped unceremoniously back onto the dreadful excuse for a chair.

Trainers at the Company never answer workers' questions directly and most boys learn soon not even to ask. Work Skill training's most important lesson for Henry was about to be learned. #71 pressed the blue button on her control pad and filled the boy's ass with a significant electrical charge.

#3-729 tried to jump out of the chair but the hook held him down. The boy attempted to wriggle away from the burning jolts, but the metal chest restraint allowed no side-to-side movement. Locked into place, the new hire stomped his feet, screamed loudly and wriggled his ass in vain attempts to escape the torture that was breaking loose inside his ass.

His Trainer tapped a few notes onto her tablet, made sure a full description of the spectacle was recorded and then spoke into his headphones.

"Build an introductory page for the survey." She focused again on her tablet, watched his reactions, and entered a few more observations.

"Damnit to hell!" he screamed into unhearing air and re-focused on the screen to get the damned intro page done and be released from the agony in his asshole. He typed and clicked, reworded, and aligned and finally built a respectable survey introductory page. Announcing once again that he was done, Henry began to stand.

She tapped her blue button again and the boy immediately shrieked in pain. He was bouncing and foot-stomping, screaming, and wriggling but in the end, he remained exactly where he was with his aching ass planted securely on the bondage chair. Then he saw a new screen on his monitor.

His next assignment was described in detail. #71 measured how long it took the boy to read it and begin working.

Henry was livid about the entire situation even though building webpage after webpage was in his blood. It was not the actual work that bothered him; rather, it was the damned chair and the nerve of that women to inject so much pain into his rectum when he could not even see her do it. Or do anything to stop it.

And that's when #3-729 learned how boys work at the Company. They are told what to do and they do it without questions or breaks. And if they do not perform, their asses are fired upon by a simple blue button that every woman supervisor can – and will – press. Through his tears, #3-729 read his next assignment and Henry began to work. The assignment never mattered; what #3-729 had to learn had just been accomplished.

Training Oliver to Work

The new staff hires with technical skills were often the first to receive Work Skills training, so #67 dragged the leashed #6-437 to its training compartment where he was plunked onto an uncomfortable work bench. His Trainer secured the lock on the chains attached to the chair and she then took her place on a platform in front of him while the training software booted up.

In his former world, Oliver was used to configuring and maintaining cutting edge security tools. In this new world, he had to learn the very few programs and tools he did have access to – and which bleeding edge tools that did not – and how he would perform his assignments. The Intake Team knew that security workers were control freaks and preferred that they manage powerful firewalls, switches, and routers by themselves. At the Company, such important tasks were never assigned to male workers.

#67 read his first assignment into his headset. "Patches and updates," she said.

He was happy to be relieved of the agony of First Training and having endured a sporadic night's sleep on cold concrete, Oliver was almost happy to have something that he excelled at to do. Ignoring #67's simple instruction because he knew better than she did – better than most others in his department, especially women – what was needed, he clicked open the configuration screens and began downloading patches and updates.

Within seconds, his ass blew up in pain.

Trainers called it the "Work Skills Dance," when new hires reacted to torture that only they could feel. Males worked in concentric circles on risers that sported side panels that blocked their view of other workers. In addition, boys wore eyewear that allowed them to look only straight ahead. Trainers knew that layout forced them to focus.

When a boy's ass was shot with electricity and it began doing the Work Skills Dance, no male saw it; it was visible only to all the woman supervisors in the room. Workers were carefully monitored all day, every day, and boys like the one formerly named Oliver and now named with a leading #6 were scheduled for daily punishment to reinforce their specific Work Skills. They did not comprehend yet that meant every day for the rest of their lives. They would get it soon.

Being punished every day was to become #6-437's new normal and when fully trained, would come to look forward to it and long for it if it were withheld. Many of the security engineers hired at the Company were likewise given a "6" prefix. It seemed to the Trainers that daily punishment and computer security went hand-in-hand. Trainers showed them that once they discovered the most effective punishment for each of them and they made sure they tasted it daily. It was something about their personalities and needing daily reminders of what their lives had become that helped Trainers choose their punishments, which were later evaluated and approved by the CEO.

It often took a few years before new hires eagerly anticipated their daily punishments.

"You began without instructions," #67 said. "Listen well the first time. We do not repeat instructions at the Company."

Oliver tried to explain that he did not expect her to repeat his assignment because it was clear enough and he wanted to get on with it but another jolt pierced his ass. As he did the Work Skills Dance while seated firmly on the uncomfortable work bench, his screen displayed "FAILURE" in bold red letters with a "Next" button below.

Oliver was outraged that he failed a routine server patch exercise because of something as minor as a second line of instructions when he knew how to do the task with his eyes closed. Desperately wanting to go back a screen and finish the first task, he tapped every keystroke combination he could think of to force it to display the prior screen. #67 watched in amusement as the boy fought for control, a feeling he would never experience again.

"Your next job," she started quietly while watching Oliver's fingers press one last keystroke and then rest on the keyboard in submission. "Repel a DDoS attack." She took a breath to see if he would wait for the rest of her instructions before starting and with careful Intake and Training teamwork, he did.

"Build a plan for the router manager to execute."

If it were possible, Oliver became even more outraged. Write a program for a superior router manager? Why did not he have full router control? It was much simpler for him to reconfigure the routers and build broad IP address blocks if he could do it his own way. Doing it this way would take more time, and worse, would mean that someone else would be able to edit his plan and even change his counterattack. When he opened his mouth to complain, #67 jabbed the blue button. Not one syllable fell from his lips when the crazed dance of pain shook his entire body.

His Trainer watched the boy spasm in agony and try mightily to bolt from his unbreakable locks. Every time the boy lifted his ass an inch from the workbench, he was forced to plop it down again harder, an exercise that helped spread the rectal jolts more deeply throughout his lower body. Most boys figured it out quickly, but Oliver seemed to be a very slow learner.

They eventually learn, the CEO taught. For fast success, repeat punishment without warning.

That's what #67 did for the entirety of #6-437's Work Skills Training day. The new boy would have to be watched carefully and punished daily to shed its habit of failing to learn in a timely manner. Speed and accuracy were every boy's requirement and its work for the Company was its only focus for the rest of its life.

Training Cory to Work

Administrative staff enforced the Company's rules and policies, made sure workers conformed to Company processes and also kept tabs on their other-world disappearances to assure former co-workers and families that they were safe. Boys like Cory were never allowed to see or hear outside news or learn what communication had been exchanged between the Company and their former employers or limited families. Human Resources provided just enough updates to pacify outsiders that all was well and usually, within a few months, the few communications ceased. Their former lives were forgotten.

For the new hires, this process was designed to reinforce to them that they had never lived another life. Choosing new hires with few or no pesky relationships was always a Company imperative.

Led by #54 to a small compartment with a binder full of rules for male workers, Cory was positioned on a low red workbench. When his Trainer leaned in to lock him in place, his eyes ran up and down her long blonde hair that was cascading over her shoulders. #54 was selected intentionally by the Intake and Training groups to walk him so that she could measure his distractibility and eliminate it. Company boys were not allowed to focus on anything except the work assigned to them.

Stepping onto the platform in front of him, #54 noticed that he turned his head slightly to see where she had gone. The raised tier system was one method used to remind boys that women supervisors were always higher in position to them, including the workday. They could observe the workers but lighting hid the women from their view. Boys were kept naked and women staffers wore clothing befitting their position. Nakedness subdued thoughts of the outside world or escape by boys, and in time, they came to see their nakedness as their normal. In this training exercise, #54 was dressed similarly to all Trainers on the train trek: leather vest, leather thong and thigh-high leather boots. The CEO thought leather was amusing but the girls liked it, even the fat ones, so the CEO made it their uniform.

Besides, when the CEO wanted to use her girls, she had quick access to all the parts that interested her. One nipple – the branded one – was always in plain sight. It was easier for the CEO to remember their staff levels that way. She was too busy to memorize their numbers.

"Assignment," she said because boys always need their attention focused with simple, clear language. "Review the policies for Company boys during work hours. A test is required for any boy to rise to the next level."

Cory was amused that he had to take a test after all the years he had as a manager in Human Resources and the promotions he had earned. He knew personnel procedures backward and forward and assumed he would ace whatever test they threw at him. That way, he could move on to a higher level with more responsibility. And get a better chair. He flipped open the binder, found the "Work Hours Behavior" tab and started reading the two-page document.

He saw the monitor flash and turned to look. Nothing appeared on the screen, so he continued reading. Then it flashed another time and it drew his attention to the screen again.

The monitor flash test showed #54 that the boy was too easily distracted and that would negatively impact his work for the Company. Boys are expected to pay 100% attention to their assignments, complete them and move directly to the next one, thereby producing more finished work for the Company. Work Training was the beginning of teaching new hires how to focus.

On the third screen flash, Cory again turned his attention to the monitor and as soon as he did, #54 pressed her tablet's turquoise button. The ever-present Company ring that boys wore around their genitals was the target of that button. The turquoise button #54 pressed made the ring tighten and Cory yelped with fear that his cock and balls were being amputated by the metal band. Like most new boys before him, he spread his legs to examine more closely what was happening to his penis and balls. But it was when he reached for his cock and balls with one hand that was supposed to be working on an assignment that #54 taught him a new Work Skill he obviously needed.

Then she pressed the yellow button and gel shot from the cock ring/ It sprayed his genital area with fast-drying substance that shrank as it mixed with air. Cory screamed as it tightened and when he attempted to use his hands again, she pressed the violet button. The cock ring and sac tightened brutally and his genitals felt as if they were on fire.

Cory was terrified that blood would stop flowing to his cock and balls and they would wither, die, and fall off.

The boy could scream his lungs out and #54 still would neither care nor react. Trainers at the Company learned how to ignore trivial male noises and her only thoughts were how fast #7-650 returned his attention to the task. The 7's needed very close supervision and #54 kept an eye on this one's every movement. She applied a swift electronic correction each time the boy erred. The 6 in his new name called for strict daily punishment and the zero, which every Trainer was familiar with, meant that to train the boy to be effective in Work Skills, she would begin Company-mandated penis exclusion training sooner than the other Trainers did with their new hires.

She neither pressed the purple button during this Work Skills training session nor released the shrunken bag's tension. #54 decided that he was likelier to learn more effectively if he endured it for the entire session and if he did not progress fast enough, perhaps for the rest of his work life. It was simply a choice she could make if she believed it would train the boy faster and better.

With a short tap on the blue button, she shot only a single jab into his anus. He stared at the monitor and with palpable effort, started typing his responses to the test. If he grimaced while typing, #54 did not see it. If he were scared that his cock would shrivel up and fall off, she did not concern herself about it. The only thing that mattered was that he completed the task correctly and began the next item on his list. After all, the never-ending job was what the rest of his life would entail, and it is what every boy at the Company strived to complete. Even though they knew there would always be a next assignment, worker boys always hoped against hope there would be an end sometime. It just never happened.

Over time, each move that got him to start and complete the next job became every boy's only goal. "Time off" was a distant memory.

When he clicked the submit button on the screen, the next task appeared and Cory searched the documentation and answered the on-screen questions. All the while, the boy's cock and balls were squeezed with increasing force and each time he leaned in to click another submit button and groaned in pain, #54 smiled.

Trained boys understand the next task is their only job. They do not remember yesterday, and they are not concerned about tomorrow.

Her trainee, a big black former sports hero, had been trained in Work Skills in record time and had now turned into #7-650 forever. She checked the timer and noted on her tablet that it had taken only 1 hour and 10 minutes to break him in. She released the cock pressure and Cory resisted the overwhelming urge to grab and comfort his cock and balls from their torture. But he saw the word "Next" on the screen with an arrow, took a deep breath, and clicked it.

Training James to Work

Although James had prison-level plumbing skills, the new hire now known as #2-273 was scheduled to be trained in various Company repair areas and if the boy succeeded, he might be allowed to learn how to move up to installing upgrades in the future. Maintenance was the lowest professional level that the Facilities staff had and being allowed to perform upgrades was a dream among them. The CEO was fond of adding new features to facilitate her staff's routines and water-related fixtures were always a top priority. Only a select few were allowed to see them and fewer to work on them.

When #62 led James to his Work Training station, the Programming Team had just finished installing a large touchscreen monitor because James's computer skills were almost non-existent. The background reports revealed that he did not read much in prison, sought no further degree but managed to attend all the career and technical education programs offered during his sentence. That path was how he became a certified plumber. The CEO had one opening in a remote outpost for which he was designated unless he proved more useful at HQ.

Without instruction, James sat his naked ass on the tiny stool, spread his legs and waited silently. *Prison behavior*, #62 thought. But at the Company, every learned response was to be erased from new hires, so it was time for James to learn and adapt to the Company way. Besides, he would be working at the Company for the rest of his life, so there was no better time to start than now.

With a tap on an orange button, a jolt of unexpected pain shot up through James's ass and his body reacted and tried to shoot up from the seat. The bench's low level and his rapid movement caused him to fall toward the floor and crunch his body into a fetal ball as if he were back in prison and another prisoner were going to attack his ass or cock. His Trainer knew this ingrained behavior would never do. New hires were prohibited from bringing old behaviors to the Company. As a plumber, James did not need to be locked into a chair. He had to learn obedience on two feet.

She ordered him to his knees and James complied despite his pain and without asking a single question.

"Instructions!" she snapped at him and eyed him up and down.

Despite his agony, James understood. He hung his head in silence and fought the urge to comfort his painful asscheeks. She made him kneel silently for three full minutes before issuing her instructions. He fidgeted once or twice and #62 noted that on her tablet.

At last, she gave me a command to follow. "Sit," she said. And James positioned himself on the frightening little seat.

The screen flashed the word "Begin," but James did not reach for the button that blinked on the big monitor because she had not ordered him to touch it. He remained motionless while waiting for her instruction, which for James, had become commands that he dare not disobey.

With a terse "Start" command, she watched him look at the screen and press icons representing tools he would need to complete various jobs. Workers' time was better spent repairing or maintaining toilets and shower sprays, enema hoses and emptying the pits. If they were adept at pre-packing their tools for each job, the systems were kept in good order with no wasted time.

The next test was one the Trainers always enjoyed: having new maintenance staff work on plumbing while naked boys were struggling to shit on command. If a worker could not separate the job from gawking at shitting workers, he would never succeed at the Company. #62 started the video and waited for James to click the icons that would determine his fate.

The screen displayed video of groups of boys sitting on the small toilets and placing their feet on the tall benches all the while struggling to keep their knees together for no other reason than the Company demanded it. One after another, the groups shit and a strong order permeated James's work cubicle. Each time a group finished and was hosed off, the smell grew. Finally, the screen showed a struggling boy empty his bowels and press the flush button and nothing happened. No flush. No bell alerting his superiors that he had performed. The boy was in a state of panic that he had performed and there was no proof!

James realized that the toilet was broken.

The video zoomed in on the trembling boy. His tangible fear was that without the bell that signaled a successful dump, his entire group would be punished for his failure to shit on cue.

If one fails, they all fail. All are punished for every failure. That was Company policy and was always obeyed.

James's screen froze and he saw the tool icons come into focus. He understood that his job was to fill his toolkit with what was needed to fix the toilet. With so many icons to choose form, he was torn between tapping icons and waiting for his Trainer to tell him to do so. This was a standard Company dilemma: should the worker move quickly to do the job, or should he wait for a superior's direct instruction? James chose to wait.

#62 nodded to herself and knew that this boy would be one of her many training successes. After only one full day on the train and a short morning lesson, she owned him. He was not her first felon but the first whose conviction was for the violent rape and degradation of a woman. His training plan would make him remember every day that his crimes were unforgivable and that he was to become the abused prisoner he tried to make of his rape victims. #62 smiled as she added another category of accomplishments to her record.

Training Evan to Work

In unusual pre-train preparations, the CEO supervised the preparation of Evan's Work Skills training module herself with only minor input from the teams. She knew that this new hire required customized training because when she reviewed the secret audio, video, and phone tap footage, she recognized how his disruptive intent could cause disruption at Company HQ. Worse, she recognized that his cavalier attitude, especially toward women, was a worse offense than his underhanded unspoken interest in adding her company to his hedge fund buyouts of businesses that he bought and then decimated.

She intended to solve both of his drawbacks before trying to predict if and when his "8" might be carried out. Company staff understood that the 8's never returned to the outside world, even after retirement. Evan's future was ordained from the moment he answered the want ad – he would stay at the Company forever either as an intact worker or as a eunuch – and he was the only one who did know it. Yet. But he would be provided an inkling during his Work Skills training this morning. The CEO wondered if he were smart enough to figure it out.

When #36 led the boy to the training car for his Work Skills session, she exuded a warm glow of confidence that was a result of her own significant training that was devised to deal with this 8-designated male. It was not often that boys like Evan made it all the way to the Company HQ when their disrespectful attitudes were revealed on First Day. #36 recalled only two others with similar personality faults – one was sent off the train naked and penniless on a dreary platform in a small town in the middle of a rainy night and the CEO never mentioned the boy again after issuing her expulsion order. The second time involved a fat arrogant Asian boy that spat at #67, who immediately rammed an electrified sound into the boy's little cock's pee hole and pressed the rarely used red button.

Red buttons were saved for when the most severe punishment during training was required, a result the Asian boy had surely earned.

Within seconds, the chubby boy was sprawled on the concrete floor, writhing and screaming his lungs out from the rapid shots of electricity that set his stubby penis on fire. #67 tapped the red button again to end the penalty and waited for the boy to recognize his unacceptable behavior and see if he could learn never to do that again. Instead, he spat at her a second time and she immediately held her finger on the red button until he passed out screaming in agony, wasted sounds that no one heard.

That evening, the CEO reviewed the day's videos and saw his double infractions. She ordered him expelled with the blunt phrase, "Throw his fat ass off my train."

He was forced off the train in the middle of the night, naked, hands locked behind him, with no identification except for a ten-dollar bill rolled up and sticking out of his little cock's hole at whatever station happened to be next on their route. She had the training rod that was shoved up his ass left in place. The CEO never mentioned him again, either.

But Evan had made it through First Day by submitting to the small morning exercise with the females' auditions. As a result, #67 began the boy's special Work Skills training in earnest because the consequences – whether he passed or failed – were filled with lifelong outcomes for this new hire. Although the staff understood that an occasional set of genitals would be sliced off, none of them wanted it on their record that their trainees failed training and were shoved into the eunuch dorm at the Company. That fate set a cloud over the trainers' skills and worked against their own promotions.

The three-sided work cubicle was lit by an overhead fluorescent lamp that reflected vividly on the seat's red vinyl cover. Evan stared at the surroundings – a small seat, tiny desk and large monitor, certainly nothing like the ergonomic setup in his own private office. #67 eyed him and then looked at the seat and Evan sat down. She locked him in place and tapped her tablet to open a small hole in the bench directly under Evan's ass. From the front, a hard plastic tube emerged, whirred forward and up and she snapped it closed to completely obscure the cock and balls that Evan was so fond of caressing.

She locked a noise-cancelling headset over his ears and rendered him completely immobile, deaf to the world, ass open and ready, and penis locked away. All within nine seconds. #67 tapped her tablet and recorded the almost-record time.

"Run a cost-benefit analysis," she said.

Evan attempted to turn his head toward the disembodied voice of the Trainer on the platform in front of him, but the locks and cock cage cut off any movement. Instead, he saw the screen fill with data and he instinctively reached for the keyboard. Cost-benefit analysis? He could do them in his head, no matter what size the company or project. Via the overhead cameras, the CEO saw him smirk.

As Evan read the data and worked through the spreadsheet's projections, his satisfied smile faded. There were numbers relating to food costs, housing allowances and medical expenses. The income data displayed the value of the services rendered, specifying massages, nail treatments, hair styling and several female esthetic services. One expense caught his eye: "Castration Costs." All the column headers were similar: "Costs of Keeping 8's" and "Benefits of Keeping 8's." He figured out that "8's" were employees that were castrated and whose maintenance costs far outweighed their retail value. It hit him like a ton of bricks: he was evaluating whether or not to keep male geldings who cost a Company more than they brought in.

But what collided in his brain was that it was that the methodology was the same analysis he built and used repeatedly when buying businesses that he wanted to tear apart and resell. He recognized the algorithms and knew that he had customized some of them himself. How the hell did they get his data? As an untrained boy, he simply could not help himself.

"Where did you get this?" he demanded.

Instead of an answer that no boy ever deserved at the Company, #67 used the purple button to discharge gel directly from the rod that had slide up into his ass. She watched Evan screech in familiar purple-level pain. He did the dance that all the Trainers found so amusing where the boys found themselves locked in the struggle against their locked chains, and in this case, caged cock and balls, in useless attempts to escape the torture. In Work Skills training, no boy would leave the training area until its Work Skills training was complete. #67 smiled as she ignored Evan's louder screeching.

It took almost 45 seconds before the pain subsided enough for Evan to refocus on his task. Through gritted teeth, he studied the spreadsheet and reviewed the column totals and row variables.

"Analysis," #67 stated. It was not a question.

Evan drew in a big breath and replied, "They're not making you any money."

"Incomplete," she said.

Evan took another deep breath and said through clenched teeth, "Get rid of them."

The Trainer noted the time on her tablet and watched the camera as the big monitor previewed a single sentence. "You are an 8," it said. She heard him gulp in horrified understanding. He had just recommended his own castration and expulsion order! And for the duration of the train trek, Evan knew that at any moment he could be neutered like a gelding and have to exist somewhere with others like him, a group that he had just evaluated to be unnecessary, too expensive to keep and very dispensable.

#67 tapped a few notes into her tablet as Evan stared at the cage covering his cock and tried to fight the urge to rescue his penis from a horrifying fate even though he knew all he could touch was hard plastic. He needed to feel his penis, rub the shaft, hug the balls, and let the glow of erection fill his body again. The Trainer smirked and pressed the red button again but this time, with the genitals it hid still attached to a body.

They will not be there for long, she predicted.

Chapter 30

Capping off the second – and last full day – of training, the new hires revisited the skills they learned on First Day. The CEO believed repetition and constant practice produced consistent results among all types of new hires. She demanded dependable and steady production from her staff. Deviation from any Company rule was not tolerated.

In mid-afternoon, the new hires were sent to the toilet room for required peeing. Unsurprisingly, they all performed on cue. If any of them was afraid of peeing in public, that had been eliminated through sheer desperation. Every bathroom exercise was performed on schedule and would be withheld if new hires required a behavior reminder. The Trainers were amused when they passed by a lineup of naked boys jiggling up and down so as not to drip pee before they were permitted *to toilet*, the Company verb. When a boy could not control himself, he was forced to lap up his incontinence in front of the entire training staff, who made sure boy staffers could watch. From time to time, the CEO would order all the new hires to flatten themselves in the spilled pee and roll around in it.

They behave better when they understand the consequences. Make them experience the consequences firsthand. All of them at once.

For practice, the group was marched to dinner and presented with the minimum required nutrition to keep them in good enough shape to do the Company's work. Fat boys were put on diets and skinny ones fed high-calorie protein drinks to bulk them up enough to work long shifts without breaks. This time, they gobbled up whatever was put in front of them and none of them could remember when his last real meal had been. They returned their trays and cleaned their tabletops and seats with disinfectant spray that reminded them of two things: clothing was not furnished for them and their assholes were unacceptably dirty.

After a full Second Day of training, the new hires were put to bed. With an upcoming morning full of chores to ready the train's occupants for arrival at Company HQ, boys needed whatever rest they could get on the cold cell floors. The CEO watched the Trainers put them to bed them live on her monitors and the Trainers knew they were being observed. Each of them threw her full effort into what would become the boys' nightly ritual throughout the rest of their lives at the Company.

All boys were put to bed at the same time and always in the same way.

They need constant reminders that they are equally subservient. None has any privileges, no matter what job it performs.

Before bed, the boys were marched to toilet and each was instructed to empty his bowels. Shitting on command was the simplest way to remind the new hires that even the most personal task is no longer private for them. They had to learn that every boy performs its assigned task when ordered to do so. At the Company HQ staff wing, known as the barn, the male staff was scheduled toilet time prior to bed. They are sent in large groups each night so that there is no "low level" group or "supervisor group." Such designations do not exist for males at the Company.

A post-dinner thick drink was compulsory and Medical made sure each boy's bowels were eager to shit within 15 minutes. It took a few days for the correct dosage to be devised for new boys, but Medical always succeeded. It was the rare boy whose bowels screamed for toileting outside of the regular schedule.

The Trainers reinforced the males' no-caste status every day. Especially at shit time. Boys learned quickly that every bodily function belonged to the Company and they were never allowed to change their routines. They had no good or bad days. They just had days.

"Sit," a distant voice said through the speaker. The five of them sat simultaneously.

"Shit," the disembodied voice commanded.

Five boys strained and pressed their asses to force something – anything – out of their rectums. Two of them grunted, much to the CEO's amusement, and one leaned back for a better angle. Huffing and struggling, they worked their lower bodies to produce even a single ball of shit because they were told to do so by an anonymous voice on a speaker. The "shit dance," a Trainer dubbed it and it caught on.

Watching them struggle to shit on command, the CEO knew they were all eventually trainable. But Evan's behavior caught her eye.

Eyes closed and palms flattened on the little toilet seat, Evan pressed down and rose slightly before pressing again. Up and down, ever so slightly, again and again. She had seen it before and knew exactly what she wanted her staff to do to cure this behavior.

Eyeing #41, she had her deliver a message to #36. Within moments, she entered the toilet area, grabbed Evan off the toilet and put him on his hands and knees in front of the still fighting-to-shit group. She pressed a syringe into his ass and shot in a wad of lubrication. With a flourish, she inserted a long tube that was connected to a bag of hot fluid that the Company used to compel boys' rectums into behaving on cue. She pressed the bag flat in a single squeeze and the solution discharged into Evan's ass.

No one cared about his screeches. None of the Trainers paid attention to his writhing on the floor. No one focused on his hot ass that was screaming to be emptied.

#36 pulled the tube out of his ass and inserted a fat plug to keep the contents stopped up. The CEO knew Evan's dirty little secret and would put him on a public enema schedule and fiber-filled diet that Medical would supervise.

Learn their filthy little secrets. Use them to control the boys. Workers must learn that you own their bodies, souls, and fears.

After every other boy had finished and was hosed off, they were arranged in a circle surrounding him. Evan collected himself only enough to beg to be allowed to use the toilet. The CEO watched with curiosity as her Trainer correctly ignored his pleas. He begged. He groveled. She stared at him while he beseeched her, implored her, supplicated himself and then did exactly what the CEO predicted would happen next.

He cried.

At that moment, the CEO knew that she owned him, body and soul and fear.

Having seen all she cared to observe, the CEO flicked off her monitors and had dinner delivered to her private car. The red wine was beautifully aged and delicious.

Chapter 31

The CEO enjoyed the end of each train trek and off-loading the new hires to the Company's remote headquarters. A small bridge was the harbinger of the final leg of the journey and she knew that staff from all divisions would be in place at the station to disembark the Teams, support workers. Trainers. and last, the new hires.

The CEO always exited the train first. Only special staff members were allowed in her presence and were assigned to take care of her needs. Workers would later swarm onto the train in silence and begin cleaning, sterilizing, and restocking. The IT crew downloaded the video to ready it for editing for the CEO's later review.

Just prior to arrival, the Trainers woke the boys and marched them to the toilet area for peeing, occasional shitting and a solid hosing that used several long-handled scrub brushes and gobs of disinfectant soap. Walking them in line through hot blowing air, the boys were dried off and led to a narrow windowless aisle that led to Company Intake tube. Two ankle cuffs with a steel bar between them were locked to their ankles and a massive clamp was attached to the center of each steel bar.

When the speaker's voice instructed, the Trainers opened the outside door. There was a woosh of an airlock breaking and without warning, the boys were dragged by their ankle bars off the train and lifted upside down into total darkness. The Trainers pivoted on their boot heels, walked away, and attended to their arrival duties. Their job for this trek was complete.

On the other wide of the airlock, five new hires were suspended, inverted in total darkness as liquid shot from every direction and soaked them everywhere. They felt, but could not see, brushes that scrubbed them inside and out. Unseen hands pulled their asses apart and enemas were discharged into their assholes and were followed by plugs that kept the burning enemas – laced with *fire* – in place. Opaque goggles were wrapped around their eyes while five penises were covered with plastic cages. Their nipples were clamped and if they screamed in pain or even in horror, no one heard or cared.

At another locked door at the end of a different aisle on the train, the Company's Female Intake process began.

On the train, the new females who successfully auditioned earlier were led naked toward the exit specifically for new females. Their huge bosoms that were on the CEO's must-have list were marked by a Sharpie with their temporary numbers. Staff herded them into the intake area where each was to be housed until their personnel records were entered. Intake staffers updated their records and deposited the women with each one's specific Intake team. They would be brought into the Company processes before the CEO would assign them as trainees to the Trainers she preselected for them. And everyone would learn exactly how long the new women would last.

Unbeknownst to the women, the CEO already decided which areas she wanted them trained. She assigned them to Company sectors she was beginning to develop. One woman was assigned to each area: Ass Insertion, Esthetics Hair Removal, Medical Branding, Psych Control and Eunuch Usage.

New females at the Company provided video entertainment for the CEO and her selected Trainers as the new females learned how they were required to submit before they could attempt to study how to make absolute submissives out of males. Some could eventually rise in the ranks to become Special Trainers who handled Company staffers that needed corrective punishment. Their work – and the rest of their lives – had just begun.

The Trainers were always the last to leave the train to make way for the cleaners, stockers and mechanics who inspected the Company train from top to bottom after every trek. Every inch of the train was examined, and the train was readied for its next trek with Trainers and new hires when the Company needed new skilled staff.

Only then would the CEO run another want ad.

Chapter 32

Bent in half with their asses spread wide, their voices shrieking insanely through gagged mouths and their bodies spasming in delightful synchronicity, their antics were ignored by Company Medical staff, who pierced the five new hires just below their cock and balls. The staff attached electronic rings and locked them permanently in place. They initialized the microchips to track them. From her vantage point, the CEO nodded in approval.

She always kept a constant eye on her entire staff via a multi-monitor setup. She enjoyed new hires' mass piercing and subsequent branding because piercing showed that the Intake process was about to begin in earnest. The train trek was over and the new boys – and a few new females – were ready to begin joining her Company's ranks.

The CEO's iron fist of ownership gripped the entire staff. During the Company's 20-year history, no boy had ever escaped. No matter how they tried, the CEO had permanent GPS on all of them and knew how to deal with instigators.

APPENDIX

The Company and Staff

Intake Team	Training Staff
#33 Chloe, handles Cory	#54 Cory's Trainer
#46 Cassandra, handles Henry	#62 James Trainer
#38 Casey, handles Oliver	#71 Henry's Trainer
#55 Claudia, handles James	#67 Oliver's Trainer
#43 Cara, handles Evan	#36 Evan's Trainer
Technical Staff	**Company Sectors**
#82 chemical developer	Intake Team
#94 insertion expert	Medical & Nutrition Division
#88 esthetician and hair removal	Psychological Team
#58 new women trainer	Training Staff
#72 expert whipper	Esthetics Department
#41 tech manager	Engineering/Developers
#47 equipment trainer	
#34 Sybil, top staffer	
New Hires	**Company Owner**
James, ex-con rapist	
Cory, HR manager	The CEO
Henry, web developer	
Oliver, security engineer	
Evan, venture capitalist	

ABOUT THE AUTHOR

Amity Harris is the author of the best-selling Femdom novels *Debbie's Gift* and *The Training Farm* and has written first-person Femdom stories about her life for decades. Many of her stories are available on her website, *Amityworld.com*. One of the community's best-known and original online writers of Female Domination erotica, Amity Harris has made many of her stories and novellas available to the BDSM community for free.

Her plots are compelling, and her characters are complicated. In *Debbie's Gift*, Ron's story is that of strict training with male overseers and a mysterious Mistress whose facility for training is macabre and most importantly, successful for the women who want well-trained slaves and slave-husbands. In the novel, *The Training Farm*, Amity moves into a world where 245 males are converted into the animals they were meant to be and sent home after successful training with fierce competition to perform for their owners as perfectly trained slaves.

All of Amity Harris's work is available at Amazon in eBook and print formats.

Amity lives the life she writes about and that makes her tales all the more real for her readers who understand that they are reading the work of a Dominant who lives the life of a slave-owning Mistress and enjoys the males and females she owns, trains, and enjoys for her personal use.

Visit Amity at her website: https://amityworld.com

Printed in Great Britain
by Amazon